To the Green Mountains

BOOKS BY ELEANOR CAMERON

The Mushroom Planet Books
The Wonderful Flight to the Mushroom Planet
Stowaway to the Mushroom Planet
Mr. Bass's Planetoid
A Mystery for Mr. Bass
Time and Mr. Bass

Other Books for Children
The Terrible Churnadryne
The Mysterious Christmas Shell
The Beast with the Magical Horn
A Spell Is Cast
A Room Made of Windows
The Court of the Stone Children
To the Green Mountains

Novel
The Unheard Music

Essays
The Green and Burning Tree: On the Writing
and Enjoyment of Children's Books

TO THE GREEN
MOUNTAINS
by Eleanor Cameron

E. P. DUTTON & CO., INC.   *New York*

Library of Congress Cataloging in Publication Data

Cameron, Eleanor   To the green mountains

SUMMARY: A young girl growing up in a hotel in a
small town in Ohio is overcome with desire to reach
a much longed-for home in the mountains, remembered
since she was four.

I. Title.
PZ7.C143To   [Fic]   75–6758   ISBN 0–525–41355–3

Published simultaneously in Canada by Clarke,
Irwin & Company Limited, Toronto and Vancouver

Designed by Riki Levinson
Printed in the U.S.A.   First Edition
10 9 8 7 6 5 4 3 2 1

For Ian, with love

. . . facing a fact until it divides you through
the heart and marrow like a sword . . .

—ALFRED KAZIN

Contents

1 🌿 From the Height

The silence that holds in it the hum of myriad invisible insects speaks to her of the absence of any human but herself in all these miles upon miles of forest. She has an intimation not only that she is alone in this vast solitude but that she is lost, yet knows at the same time without the least doubt that she has climbed this path before and has come to her longed for destination. No, she cannot say that. Rather, she has looked down upon it, though always the moment of actual arrival has been denied her. She lifts her head and recognizes the outline of that ridge above her, the bosses of rock on either hand, the patterns they make against the sky. She feels, as she takes turn after turn of the path, that her feet have gone this way at other times and know intimately the lay of it as it ascends.

Yet the sense of despair continues and she cannot fathom whether it is rooted in the fact that this time she is possibly lost for good, or that she will not, in any case, in the end, be given what she is struggling toward: the welcome she desires above all else. She rests for a moment and looks up the dizzying height of the pines to where their tips pierce the blinding sky. Or would they be firs, cedars, spruce? She loves these names with a peculiar intensity, and the fragrance of their sun-baked needles, for she has waited since she was little to smell that fragrance again. (A sense of confusion. Waited since she was little? But she knows this path—yes, and at different seasons: once in winter, for it seems to her that there was snow and that these trees were hung with Christmas ornaments.) And she would love the solitude and the tiny, incessant hum of insects—which is to her the sound of silence—if it weren't that she is lost.

She gets up and with bruised fingers grasps at the rocks, her feet scrabbling for one toehold after another, and comes at length to a height over which streams a cool and gentle wind. She runs across the springy carpet of needles toward a pure, clear stretch of sky swept by winds from the sea in which a lone hawk tilts and planes, then spirals away into nothingness. She is crying with relief, for she is almost there. She knows her way; she is not lost, for that stretch of sky means that the valley is just beyond, with the white house at the bottom of it.

Now here is the edge where this high saddleback drops steeply away, and there lies the valley and, in the heart of it, the spacious and airy house. And the back door opens and out comes that minuscule figure she remembers from other times, who lifts the tea cloth and shakes the crumbs from it, stands for a moment with the cloth clasped in her hands as if to take a breath, then turns and goes in and the screen door closes, but Kath cannot hear it close because the distance is too great.

She starts down the mountain, the soles of her shoes slipping on the needles, and she is sobbing with delight. . . .

And woke suddenly on the brink of bliss with her wet nightgown pasted against her body, and heard in the stifling dark the low hum of the fan behind the sheet at the foot of the bed, a sheet her mother wrung out in water every night during the breathless summer and hung on a cord stretched from one wall to the other. A sick hollow spread inside her where the hollow always spread when she was frightened or anxious or disappointed beyond bearing. She would never reach the valley and the white house and that loved figure who had gone inside to do what, Kath would never know.

She had had the dream before—how many times? Yet why should she be frightened? Frightened of what? Or perhaps the sick hollow meant disappointment, yet she felt not. Fright. And behind her closed lids saw her father standing at the door. He always unlocked and opened it without knocking, for it was his right, as if he were coming home, and nothing Mama could say made any difference. She or her mother might have been standing naked, yet he simply came and opened their door. And he would not be smiling; he was not given to smiling. He would come in; he was there, and they could make the best of it whether they would or no. But surely it would not be her father who had caused this inexplicable hollow, for he had only just gone, only two days before, and would not be in town again for another month. (She always knew how many days he had been gone; how many days before he would come again.) No, it could not be her father.

Now she saw Mama coming out of the study in that house in Columbus where they had been visiting yesterday on Mama's day off, and she had three of the big black law books in her arms, and Maizie Hammond, Mama's friend, had the other three. Mrs. Hammond came over and put these in Kath's arms, and Mama said, "Maizie, I wish you would let me pay you—" or had it been, "I wish you would let me pay you more—"? And they brought the law books back to South Angela on the train for Grant.

No, not that. Nothing there to cause the hollow. What, then? The dream? It must simply have been the dream itself, the longing for what she could not have because here they must stay, in this one room at the hotel, for there was no way out.

2 ❧ Tiss

Curled sideways halfway up that dim flight, the same step
she'd always used to sit on and in the exact same position,
she sank her teeth into the club sandwich, taking as big a bite
as she could possibly manage, then chewed with her eyes
closed in order to savor more deeply the delectable flavors of
moist thick slices of turkey, crisp bacon, tart tomato, and soft
white bread generously spread with butter. In this moment
she was seven again. For it was one of the ways Swan had
occasionally indulged her when he was in the mood: made
her these enormous club sandwiches (crub samriches, she'd
called them then, just for fun, knowing better). And she
would invariably bring them to these gloomy side stairs of
the hotel, the coolest place in summer, to feast quite privately
and quietly, out of the way of her mother's eye, emitting
little groans of pleasure that nobody would be likely to hear.
This place and this sandwich went together.

Of course in those days Swan had exacted his small price.
No doubt most people have one or more idiosyncrasies difficult of explanation, and one of Swan's was that he'd liked to
pick Kath up by the neck. You might have said that it was a
symbolic action, his way of choking the white race, yet he had
never seemed to do it with any malice nor with any secret

dislike of Kath. He had never cared who was in the kitchen so long as it wasn't Grant or Mama, and she'd suffered no ill effects. She'd been a little thin thing then, light-boned, and Swan would put his big black hands around that pipestem neck, raise her gently off the floor while she giggled and clutched his arms, hold her there for a second or two, then let her down again. That was all there was to it; it was a kind of ritual. After that she could have her club sandwich with toothpicks stuck through to hold it together and all the fixings on the side, olives and little sweet pickles and radishes cut like roses, just as he would have arranged it for a guest in the dining room.

Yes, but one day Elizabeth Rule saw him do it, pick Kath up like that. (Why had Kath never told her? But she'd never thought to! It wasn't anything—Swan had been doing it for ages.) And Mama said, fury putting a white line around her lips, that she would not *have* it. Kath could remember to this day the very moment and just how it had been. Mama's voice had trembled, her face had gone so pale as to seem transparent and her eyes went almost black. Swan just looked at Mizz Rule, straight, grave, mockingly respectful, and knew perfectly well, Mama told Aunt Lily later, that her heart was shaking, not with fear but with an enormous rage she could not fully vent because she needed him.

"Never again, Swan! Do you hear me? Never again! You might have dislocated her neck—"

"O-oh, I don't think so, Missy," he said velvetly, easily, with deep amusement. "I don't think so."

He knew, just as well as he knew what a state she was in, that she couldn't get a chef of his quality anywhere for miles around, let alone anywhere near South Angela. Traveling men, coming on from Columbus, drove till they got to South Angela Inn just because of Swan's cooking. People came in from the whole countryside on Sundays for his Sunday din-

6

ner, and vacationers always found out where to stop on their journey going through. So Mama couldn't say, "If you do it again, Swan, you're fired." At least not with equanimity. Anyhow, he hadn't done it again, only—a couple of months later he'd packed up and left without a word to anyone. That had been six years ago.

Now here he was again after all this time, quieter, no longer mocking, no longer amused. Married and divorced, he'd told Grant, and "I think we can give him another chance," Grant said to Mama, "and if there're any difficulties with drinking or temperament, I'll handle it."

Mama was a fool, Uncle Paul told her when she and Kath first came to South Angela, to think that at her age (she'd been twenty-eight then) she was capable of housekeeping a hotel full of traveling men bringing their loose women—

"Paul!" protested Aunt Lily, because this was in front of Kath.

"—their loose women," repeated Uncle Paul, his handsome face set and stubborn, "in a place with no manager but the owner who's away half the time, and full of crazy niggers who either never report on schedule or get drunk on the job and cut each other up—"

"Negroes," said Mama, not raising her voice. "I don't like the word 'nigger,' Paul, and you know it, so please don't use it in front of me again. And I have my own ideas about how to manage a hotel and how to treat the help. I'm afraid," she said lightly and indifferently, "that on this subject you and I will never agree." She studied him, her eyes holding his, then sent him suddenly the cool, teasing smile she always did when they argued, the kind she knew infuriated him. But she couldn't stand his arrogance, the way he took it for granted that because he was her brother-in-law, and her own husband was off on his failing little farm so that she had no one to turn to, he had a right to tell her how to run her life.

At any rate, one thing was true, and Mama admitted it. She could never have kept on if it hadn't been for Grant. "Grant is a treasure," she would say after some crisis in the kitchen or with the waiters or the chambermaids. In fact, Kath thought after the most recent of those terrible scenes when her father came in from his farm to stay overnight at the hotel and get more money, that Grant made him all the more—what? Shameful. Unendurable. And it was because Grant was tall and quiet and had never been known to raise his voice or lose his temper; because he had "authority," Mama called it. And her father, rather a short man, had had another of his unreasoning, childish tantrums over nothing—some unfortunate remark of Mama's about having to make ends meet when he had told her time and again he never wanted her to even hint that she was keeping him going. As for herself, she could not stand him. And it got worse each time he came. She never wanted to see him again; she prayed not to. And it had even occurred to her, after that last scene, that the way *she* felt, Grant and Tissie came right next after Mama and Grandmother and Aunt Lily, and she'd give anything to know what her father and Uncle Paul would have to say about that, when *they* weren't anywhere. Not as far as she was concerned, they weren't.

She twisted round, leaning back on her elbows on the step above, balancing her plate on her knees, and started regretfully on the second half of her sandwich. And just then Swan, with his tall white starched hat on and his long apron and with his hands stuck in his back pockets, came out of the kitchen to stand at the side door and have a smoke in the tepid air drifting through the deep-shaded screen door. Then Grant came out and they stood talking for a minute before Grant turned and happened to look up, whereupon a sudden little frown quirked his eyebrows just before Swan turned, so that Kath knew instantly her drawers were showing. Quick, she grabbed the plate, jumped up, and rattled upstairs to the second floor, along the hall to the veranda that extended along the entire front of the hotel, and let the screen door bang behind her.

Out here the burning heat of the mid-July afternoon struck through the giant sycamores. Their leaves, like hands, never stirred. In the hot afternoons—and no matter how hot it got, the sparrows kept up their monotonous cheeping—the smell of dust was strong, the dust in the street, dust on the leaves, an accumulation of it on the veranda's blackish-green wooden siding, together with the smell of horse droppings baking in the sun and the fresh, strong manure smell from a new pile near the curb.

Tonight the traveling men would sit out here, rocking and talking in the flickering dark, turning over the day's successes and failures and telling jokes that made them all burst into laughter at once and that Kath had been strictly instructed never to listen to. The wicker rockers would creak as the men shifted their weight around, tilting back in them, leaning from side to side—they *worked* those old wicker chairs—and sometimes one of them would suddenly stamp his foot if the point of some joke hit him especially hard. And the big American flag that extended over the sidewalk at the corner of the hotel would ripple and ripple its electric lights, red, white, and blue, in among the sycamore leaves all evening long until midnight. The hotel had burned down once because of lightning, and Kath was sure it had to do with the flag. In her imagination she saw the jagged sword strike out of the sky, its livid point like a fateful finger touch the rippling flag, which exploded into fragments, and the fatal charge dart through the hotel wiring so that the walls burgeoned instantly into flame. When she woke in the dark and heard thunder, saw the sudden crack of bluish-orange in the sky, she knew even now, just as when she'd been little, the thrill of dread

9

expectation and would turn and bury her face against Elizabeth Rule's shoulder.

Chewing the last bite of sandwich, she leaned her elbows on the veranda railing and looked down to see Tissie round the corner where the sign stood with the big poster on it that said UNCLE SAM NEEDS *You!* Uncle Sam, bearded and stern under his white top hat with its starred band, his lower lip protruding, stared at you, the balls of his eyes rolled up so that the dark irises met yours accusingly from under the heavy white brows and his finger pointed straight out though there were hardly any young men left in South Angela to point to, most of them being in training camps or already shipped off to France. No matter where you stood, exactly in front of him or over to the side, you were pinioned by those eyes and that finger. It was a phenomenon Kath could not understand and nobody had ever been able to explain it to her.

She chuckled and dropped a piece of crust directly in front of Tissie, lilting past on her long legs, and it caught her right on the tip of her nose and Tissie stopped, studied the crust lying there on the sidewalk, then raised her face. "You— *Buttonbox!*" she said. But she wasn't mad. She'd called Kath that the first time she'd seen her, when she was working at the hotel as a maid, and it had been Tissie's name for her ever since.

"Where y'goin', Tiss?"

"Right along here to the drugstore. Goin' to buy your mama a present."

"Be right there. I'll meet you."

The screen door banged again and Kath tore back to Mama's and her bedroom at the end of the hall, and from the bottom drawer of the bureau rooted out all the money she had saved for this occasion—forty cents. Monday would be Elizabeth Rule's birthday.

Sill's Drugstore stood next to the hotel, on the other side of the alley whose trees gave shade to that side entrance where Grant and Swan had stood talking and that Kath had looked down on while she ate her sandwich on the stairs. Clayton Sill and his wife lived at the rear. He was smaller than she, a pale, sandy, nervous, yet insinuating little man, bossed by his wife, who ran the business from behind the bead curtain that hung in the connecting doorway. What she did in the back all day no one knew, but certainly she listened, ready to emerge whenever the gossip grew too succulent not to be entered into personally and teased along with more art than Clayton possessed.

Tiss had already chosen by the time Kath arrived. She was laughing, swaying back in that willowy way she had, and she picked up her choice and showed it to Kath on her rosy palm. "One o' them little pinched-in bottles o' Devon Vi'let toilet water. Isn't that your mama's favorite?" Tissie was pleased with herself; she was in an excellent mood.

Now Kath would have to think of something else because the toilet water had been in her mind all along. She moved away, staring down at boxes of Mexican Headache Balm and Neuralgia Cure. Mama got awful headaches, but anything useful or depressing was not to be thought of. And the Princess Bust Developer, Unrivaled for Enlargement of the Bust, would be a waste of money. Mama's bust was just fine as it was, neither too large nor too small. In fact its appearance, especially when nestled behind a fall of lace on the front of a silk blouse was apt to present itself to Kath's eye as the ideal to be attained whenever she gazed despairingly at her own skimpy breasts in the mirror and wondered if they would ever be likely to amount to anything. If she could have afforded it (but the Princess Bust Developer was $1.50 a jar) she would have bought some for herself this very minute. As for the

White Rose Face Wash for Beautifying the Complexion, the Ladies Favorite Toilet Preparation, what would be the point of that when there wasn't a flaw on Elizabeth Rule's ivory skin? Thou shalt not envy thy mother's beauty. But she did, at least lately she had begun to. And if she ever forgot it, someone would be sure to speak of it. Elizabeth Rule did not appear to know she was beautiful, or perhaps she knew and did not much care under the continuous pressure and tyranny of daily life.

"—or else the doctor," Tissie was saying, "should give you a paper for something to be stirred up for Mizz Rule. She needs sustaining is my true conviction. I've mentioned Christmas Science but she says that's a religion that's all in the head and she really hasn't the time to give her mind to it. But I surely wish she would. I've known two ladies healed of complaints purely in Christmas Science and both permanent."

Now the way Tiss said "Christmas Science" made Kath realize at once that Tiss knew perfectly well what she was saying and that she had changed the name to amuse herself. But little Clayton Sill had gotten only the surface, the words, without taking in Tiss's tone, which was dry, self-teasing, her lip curled. He'd got hold of something on Tiss to tell his customers and he wasn't going to let it go. He wasn't looking at Tiss. His face crumpled and he gave a kind of squeal, leaning over the counter and shaking his head back and forth. "Christmas Science! Tissie, you're a caution. I've got to remember that one—that's the best yet. Each healing a present from the Lord."

Kath was standing close to Tiss and she looked up and saw Tiss regarding Mr. Sill's mirth with a kind of appraising gravity. Kath's eyes narrowed. She'd just remembered something.

"Mr. Sill? How do you say 'r-e-c-e-i-p-t'?"

Clayton Sill gave his head a few more shakes and then blinked at Kath. "R-e- what did you—? Oh, well, receep, I guess. Is that what you mean?"

"Re-ceep!" repeated Kath, triumphant. "That's what you always say. I've noticed you do. And it isn't 'receep.' It's 'receet.' T—not p."

The little man's face flushed scarlet, and he was just about to open his mouth when the bead curtain rattled.

"Isn't it regrettable," observed Mrs. Sill to no one in particular, "how smarty children get when they're raised in hotels. Not a place I'd be likely to bring up any child of mine in, I can tell you." She busied herself at the counter near the bead curtain, then all at once she looked up and smiled at Tissie, a small preparatory smile that drew her lips forward. "*Well*, Tissie," she said, "what's all this I hear about Grant going to be a lawyer most any day now? That was mighty nice of Elizabeth Rule to bring those big heavy law books from Columbus for him. Some sort of present, was it? I don't know any lady who'd do that for *my* husband—lug a big heavy set like that all the way back on the train."

"Well, I helped," Kath pointed out, but no one paid any attention.

Tiss had been listening without changing her position. Now she turned and studied Mrs. Sill, allowing perhaps five seconds of silence to pass before speaking.

"Well, Mizz Sill," she said at last, her tone dulcet and low, "maybe that's just your misfortune. I always did think Grant an' me was born lucky." Then she picked up her package and aired herself out—no hurry—with Kath tripping along behind. "Name o' God," she said when they were on the sidewalk, "that puts the tassel on the cap! That's the last time I go in there, I swear. I tell you, Mouse Pie, there's been times when I could knock that woman stem-winding."

"I know," said Kath. "She's always making remarks about Mama bringing me up in a hotel where dirty jokes are passed —indecent stories, she calls them—and she's always saying little pitchers have big ears as if I was five, and actually I've never listened once, or hardly ever, and then I couldn't make any sense out of them."

"Christian Science," said Tiss. "But I always liked Christmas Science best. Christmas Science is what it should be."

"Well, why didn't you tell old Sill that?"

"None o' his business! You think I care what that runty little man thinks? You think I feel called upon to explain anything to *him*?"

"No, but he'll tell everybody, Tiss. Though maybe not after what I said. He makes me sick. To think he says "bidness" for "business," and "guvmint" and "rhododendrum" and he made fun of *you!*"

They'd rounded the corner onto Elm and were going along the side of the hotel when an idea came to Kath, the idea of confiding in Tiss, and it wasn't so much to make up to her for having been insulted by Clayton Sill as because Tiss was the perfect person to tell this particular secret to. She'd turned over in her mind telling Mama because, after all, it concerned her more than anybody. It concerned *only* her, as a matter of fact, but she couldn't be certain of Mama's reaction to what she'd been up to. You'd think she could tell Chattie, which would be natural, Chattie being a close friend, but Chattie wouldn't think a thing of it. Why would she, with parents "rich as cream," Tissie called them, living in a house with two stories and Chattie having a big bedroom all her own with a screen porch in addition, and a pony and cart and everything a person's heart could desire?

As for Herb, this secret would be too suggestive. He'd been in love with her ever since she'd got into a fight for him in the first grade, and sometimes when he gave her one of those level, quiet looks of his that made her only too certain of what he was thinking, she did not know where to turn. The children had been taunting him because of his white hair and strange silvery-pink eyes, and because he was new and frightened. He was well aware from experience what would happen to him. And she could remember clearly her mounting rage at seeing him surrounded by hooting children with his hands over his face, and how her rage had got the better of her. She remembered a confused violence in which she'd charged blindly, striking out and screaming at them, "Stop it! Stop it!" because he must have seemed to her like some cornered animal. She loathed them—she could have killed them, every one of them, with their stupid faces distorted by a kind of insane glee. *"Stop it! You stop it!"* And wouldn't you think he'd have hated her after that—a girl getting into a fight for him and himself able to slip away? But, no, you could never guess how Herb would take things—never as anybody else would. And when he'd made a place for himself at school, so that he was no longer an object of torment and ridicule, his attention gradually focused itself on her and had not wavered since. She would never know what to do about Herb, with his old man's hair and his rain-gray eyes with the silvery sheen that held a rosy light in it. She could never be indifferent to him, but sometimes she thought she could not abide his love any longer.

No, Tiss was the person to tell. "Have you got to be somewhere, Tiss?"

"Not me. I aim to toe right on home an' meddle around a little an' then make me a nice strong cup o' coffee an' put my feet up."

"Well, I have something to show you. Something you're not to let on to anyone."

Tiss stopped in the middle of the pavement and gave Kath a deep look. "Are you up to some mischief, Miss Kathryn Vaughan Rule?"

"Nope. At least I don't think so. But it's the prettiest thing you ever saw—and I want one just like it. In fact, if we could save up enough money, I wish Mama could buy it. But come on, now. We can't go straight to it, because of Aunt Maud. We'll have to go around in back."

3 🌿 A Hidden Place

Kath took Tiss, puzzled and questioning, down toward the railroad tracks for three blocks, then turned left along a bushy lane and went almost as far as the back garden of Aunt Hattie and Aunt Maud and Uncle Tede Buswell. Next to the Buswells' Kath opened a stiff old gate and she and Tiss stepped into a tangle of gnarled fruit trees overgrown with honeysuckle. The burning air that oppressed the flesh in the outside world was here held off by a roof of layered leaves through which, in places, splotches of clear sunlight fell but where mostly a green golden light seeped through. Cool it was, divinely cool, and the thick shade was filled with fragrance, perhaps from roses somewhere out of sight, certainly from syringa and honeysuckle and mock orange. Little rotted apples lay in amongst the mosses and ferns and forget-me-nots and the overgrown beds of primroses and violets, past their bloom, so that an odor of decay mingled with fragrance. All was wild, rank, untended. And in among the rankness, serene as something spellbound or asleep, stood an octagonal white house surrounded by a roofed veranda.

Tiss took it all in, her mouth slightly open. She seemed to be listening. "We got no right here, Buttonbox," she said presently, "an' you know it. This is private property."

"But nobody *cares*, Tiss. Nobody cares about it. It belongs to the bank, Uncle Tede says. I asked him. All this time it's been sitting here in this jungle right next to Aunt Maud and Uncle Tede's and I never thought about it—you can't see anything from outside because of the trees. Then one day I found this gate back here and I thought—who'd care if I explored?"

Tissie lifted her skirt and on narrow, pointed slippers stepped along after Kath to a small leaning structure that turned out, when the door was forced open, to be a potting shed and storage place. In the damp, moldy-smelling interior, Kath reached in behind a row of plant pots stacked along one of the low shelves and brought up something which she held out to Tiss on the palm of her hand.

"I'll bet nobody's used this key for years and years before I found it—somebody put it there in case they forgot theirs."

"Was this what you wanted your mama to buy—a *house*?"

Kath leveled at Tiss a somber gaze. "Have you ever lived in one bedroom in a hotel year after year after year, Tissie Grant?"

Tiss's eyebrows went up and she tilted her head. "No. Grant n' me, we've always had us a house—not much, but a house, even if it wasn't much more'n a shack. An' in Georgia, Mama'n Daddy and us kids had us the nicest little place you ever saw. Not like this one here, not near as big as this, but Daddy could do anything. He was about the cleverest man I ever knew at fixing things, puttin' in lights an' cupboards an' shelves an' even windows—any kind o' windows you could want. An' Mama planted. You never did see such a garden—"

"Well, my mother and me," said Kath, "haven't ever had a house. And aren't likely to have as far as I can see, unless we go and live with Grandmother, which I want to do, but Mama won't even talk about it. Come on, Tiss. Nobody'll ever know, and we can't do any harm. There's nothing in there." They made their way through the high, juicy grass and Kath hooked her arm through Tiss's. "You know what, Tiss? I got a book from the library the other day and a couple of apples and brought them here, and I pretended this house belonged to Mama and that we hadn't moved in yet. And I really believed it." She thought about this. "Or I almost did."

"Then you are surely younger in the head than I thought, to almost believe a thing like that when you know good'n well it isn't true." Tiss paused, studying the house. "Now I recall. It appears to me this is the old Horner place. The Horner sisters lived here with a maid about as old as they was—Miss Pamela an' Miss Nonie Horner. Died within a month of each other about three or four years ago. Reminds me of Tittie Mouse an' Tattie Mouse—"

" 'If Tittie Mouse should die, Tattie Mouse would die too,' " remembered Kath from when she was little and Tiss had read it to her, so overcome with her own private view of its humor that she could scarcely get on with her reading. Once more, Tiss let out a shriek of high, delighted laughter, and Kath hissed "*Shsh-sh!*" and ran up onto the veranda, very lightly and quietly, opened the screen door, and slipped the key into the lock. "If Aunt Maud hears, she'll charge through the underbrush and drive us out. Doesn't matter if we're not up to any harm, she'd do it just to be mean, the old big-nosed—"

"Tut!" said Tissie. "That'll do."

The house was even cooler than the garden, almost cold it seemed, in comparison with the outer world. Kath ran along the dim central hall, leading spaciously from the back parlor to the front door, and Tiss swept in after her.

"Oh, it's elegant," breathed Tiss when they stood in the long drawing room on the honey-colored floor that cast its reflection up onto the low ceiling, a reflection suffused by the leaf-tinted sunlight that fell through the broad windows. The walls were papered in gray and gold and the fireplace, on the long inner wall, was of pale marble. The doors and woodwork were of some dark polished wood. "It's the prettiest room I have ever seen in my whole life." She stood quiet, her enormous eyes going from floor, to ceiling, to windows, to hearth. Suddenly she spread her arms wide. "I wouldn't cover this floor with some big old rug," she declared. "I'd have scatter rugs. An' I wouldn't have any suit o' furniture, all to match. I'd have just delicate separate pieces covered with brocade that all went together, that sort o' mingled in. An' I'd have fine lace at the windows, very soft an' fine, hangin' in nice rounded-out folds that rested onto the floor an' made little heaps of lace all along so you'd know there was plenty more where that came from an' no holdin' back."

As Tissie described, she shaped each object with her narrow hands and long, supple fingers that could curve themselves backward like the fingers of Balinese dancers. She taught Sunday school at Mount Tabernacle Baptist over in Willowtown, not so much, Mama sometimes suspected, because of any religious enthusiasm, as because she loved above all to be telling and describing, hands going, eyes shining, her upper lip rising over her white teeth and the pink interior of her full underlip revealed. Kath had noticed how Tissie's mouth, that reminded her of a tulip, cradled her words so that you enjoyed each one. Her lips moved as though they themselves had some innate awareness of each word's curious, particular value and sound, and Kath sometimes found herself watching just Tissie's mouth as she spoke.

"I think you're thinking about Chattie's house, Tiss."

"Yes, Mrs. Jameson's. There is a lady has better taste than all my other ladies put together. Those big old houses are so dark an' heavy, not light an' pretty like hers." Tissie went to certain homes over in the "good" section of South Angela up on the other side of the inn whenever teas and luncheons were given. She could make innumerable kinds of fragile sandwiches that were gone in two blissful bites, and special cookies and little pastel cakes each with a different decoration and little melting pastries filled with luscious fruit. She wouldn't have thought now of being a maid at the hotel, nor indeed anybody's maid. Furthermore, she went out only for ladies she liked best.

Tissie wandered from room to room as though furnishing this house in accord with her deepest desires built up during all that time, Kath imagined, of going to the Jamesons' and noting every single possession just as she herself had done, so that lately, within perhaps the last year or two, as the difference between her and Chattie's state was borne in upon her ever more painfully, she could hardly bear to bring Chattie to the hotel when once she had thought nothing of it—once, when they had been mere children. Now she found herself, when they were together, making some excuse to go always to Chattie's. And this was easy, and becoming almost unnecessary, because Kath realized that Chattie no longer wanted to come to the hotel.

"Don't you and Grant go sneaking this house now, Tissie," she shouted all at once to Tiss, off in another room, and giving a whirl of glee because Tissie saw what she herself had seen; felt exactly the specialness she had felt on first stealing in. "Don't you go sneaking it!"

"Sneaking *what!*" repeated Tiss in scorn. "Grant n' me'll go on living in our old two-room place 'till Judgment Day, or until it falls in on itself. Where else can the likes of us live?"

"But, *Tiss—*" and Kath crossed the hall into what must have been the library, where Tiss was standing, "—but, Tiss, that's why Mama bought—I mean *brought* the law books, so Grant can—"

21

"Won't do no good, an' you know it. It was kind an' thoughtful o' your mama, but it won't do no good."

"But why be so sure, Tiss!"

"Here in South Angela?" retorted Tiss, bored. "A lawyer? *Who for?*"

"But you could go to Columbus."

"Don't want to go to Columbus. The Willowtowners're our people an' I don't see leavin'. Know everybody here an' everybody knows us—Tiss an' Will Grant. Got no intention o' goin' to Columbus an' startin' out with nothin' in a city like that with a black man thinks he's goin' to study for the law. *On* what? An' there'll be years of it. Here we got a house an' trees an' a garden, an' Grant's got a job. There we'd be in a rat hole in some big ugly old building lookin' out on a brick wall, an' we wouldn't know a soul. I call that *death,* an' I get cold all over just thinkin' about it. But anyway," and Tiss lifted her shoulders and spread her fingers, "Grant can pleasure himself readin' an' dreamin', pretendin' he's going to *be* somethin'—pursuing his book learning," said Tiss with mocking distinctness. "Can't fix nothin' like my daddy could, but reads 'till two an' three in the mornin'. Well, I don't fool myself about that. An' now, Miss Button, I'm about to take my foot in my han' an' get out o' here. I got my waterin' to do."

Kath hid the key away behind the plant pots, and at the gate she looked up at Tiss. "Tissie, don't you think it's very strange that I dream about going back up to Grandmother's and it's always different seasons of the year? I've been there in the spring—I know it's spring because there were blossoms on her trees—and once in summer and once at Christmas. It was the strangest thing—all the firs and pines were decorated with ornaments. And I always have the hardest time getting there. I've lost my way and I get so terrified because I'm in the mountains alone and no one knows. Mama never seems to be with me. And then I begin to recognize the trail, and climbing up a certain mountain to a wide-open flat place on the top, and finally I look down into a valley and there's her house, the big two-story house with the wide lawn all the way around—"

"The way you describe it," said Tiss, "I always picture that house in my mind as some kind o' mansion, but I never gathered from your mama that your granma is 'specially well-to-do."

"I know. And I don't understand about that. I don't see how she can have forgotten the way it really is." Tiss was silent as they turned left along the lane past the back of Uncle Tede's house and two or three other backyards. Now Kath glanced up sideways at Tiss, then down again. "Tiss," she said finally, "what kind of joke is it with something about two old oars in a boat? What's funny about that?"

Tiss clucked her tongue in disapproval. "I thought your mama gave strict instructions not to listen to those jokes. So that'll just do. I don't want to hear anything more about any *boat*."

4  Grant

They parted company at Miranda and Toland, the street Tiss would take out to Willowtown. Herb and his mother lived on Toland in an ugly yellow-green house that needed painting and as Kath neared it and saw him out in the back hoeing in his mother's vegetable garden, she resolved something about the boat joke. She could say almost anything to Herb, ask him almost any sort of question as she could not Chattie Jameson (were there any point in asking Chattie questions she herself could not answer). Either Chattie's heavy eyelids would sink in disinterest or her dark, down-sloping eyes—made the more mournful by the two falls of brown hair that framed her face—would widen in shock. Once Kath had shouted in a fury, "Oh, the *bloody* thing!" and she thought Chattie was going to faint. But you couldn't shock Herb; not that she'd ever tried to. He would look at her, straight out of his silvery-pink eyes sitting back there behind his glasses, and answer her question as best he could. He took everything she said, every question or wonderment or supposition, with the utmost seriousness. If he could just cease concentrating on her, if he just weren't in love with her at an age when it was silly to be in love, he'd have made a perfect friend and she would have told him this if she thought it might do any good, but knew it would not. He couldn't help how he felt. He could cover it, but he couldn't help it, and Herb was too much himself, always, to be able to cover any feeling for long.

He saw her just as she was about to call out to him, tossed down his hoe, and came over to the fence. "Hullo, Kath. Where've you been?"

"Talking to Tiss. Herb," and they leaned, he on his side and she on hers, against the dilapidated fence Mrs. Mayhew was always after Herb to fix and, apparently because of some expression on Kath's face, he bent his head close as though he sensed their conversation was to be private, "Herb, I heard the men out on the veranda at the hotel laughing at a joke, and the end of it was something about two old oars in a boat. What's funny about that? Do you know? Tiss was disgusted with me."

His mouth, that moved and shaped itself according to whatever he was thinking, drew in and his face colored for a second then returned to its normal pallor. "Well," he said slowly, "I think they must have meant two old *whores* in a boat. That's what I think they meant, if it was that kind of a joke. But you can't really know what was funny if you don't have the rest of it."

"But, Herb, you're just repeating what I said. I mean, you haven't *explained* anything."

"Well, but I think it isn't 'oars,' but 'whores.' W-h-o-r-e-s."

"What's whores?" She said it as he had, "hores."

Herb leaned his elbow on the fence and his forehead on his open hand. "Cheap women. Women who'll be free with men not their husbands, with anybody who comes along, for pay."

"*Free* with them?"

"Yes, as if they were married."

But for *pay?* Like a *bus*iness? Kath took this in; turned it over in her mind. Such a thing would never have occurred to her. "No wonder Tiss was mad and wouldn't tell me."

"I'll always tell you anything I can, Kath."

"I know." She looked at him, thinking of his seriousness and faithfulness. "I know." And it was on the tip of her tongue to ask him to come with them, in Chattie's new wicker pony cart drawn by Little Plum out to Aunt Lily's on Monday, on Mama's birthday. Tissie had finally decided, strictly because Aunt Lily was Mama's sister, that this one more year she would help Aunt Lily clean, but only if she was to be "carried out to the farm in that new little pony cart." For Tissie, there would apparently be some special, delectable pleasure in being taken out to the country in that cart, being seen by her neighbors gathered up and carried away in such an elegant contraption. And so it was settled, and they were to have a picnic in the orchard in back of the big house. But did they have to have Herb? Did she have to ask him? There wouldn't be room for him. (Oh yes there would—right up against her on one of the two seats that faced each other in the back of the cart.) But it would be too crowded, and he probably wouldn't want to come anyway—all those women! But she knew different.

Lightly she touched his hand. "Thanks, Herb—thanks for telling me." And she turned to go. "I'll see you—"

"You were going to ask me something else."

It wasn't a question but a statement, and the words came softly and distinctly. How had he known? She had given no least hint, not that she was aware of, of what was in her mind. But Herb was uncanny. You could never fool him—or at least she, Kathryn Rule, could not. He saw into her, into her soul, she sometimes thought. "Nothing," she said, and twisted round a little, but only enough to let her gaze brush his face, then slide off again. She could not lie and look straight into his eyes. "Nothing, Herb," and she walked away with her head down and with purpose as though she had to get home. But she could feel him standing there, watching her go. She could feel what he was thinking, that she *had* been going to ask him something and maybe he even divined the reason for her not asking: that somehow it had to do with a rejection of him. At once something inside of her turned heavy and self-critical so that now she resented him for what he could do to her and was glad she hadn't asked him to come.

When she opened the door into the stifling heat of their room, Elizabeth Rule was just stepping out of the bathroom in her Japanese wrapper with her hair down her back. She always took her bath in the late afternoon so that she would be clean and fragrant to go down to dinner. She abhorred personal odors; she was always after Kath. And if some traveling man, hot and sweaty from driving in the heat on the road, came too close to her, Kath had seen her nostrils flare and how she drew back and turned aside. She was not given to touching others, laying a hand on people's arms, leaning near, kissing. One felt in her a certain reserve with all but those who were special to her like Margaret and Jack Jameson, Aunt Hattie and Uncle Tede and Aunt Lily. And when her husband put his arms around her, hungrily, after having been away from her for a month, Kath saw Mama's hands go up and press against his chest, ready to push him away if he clasped her too long or too insistently kept his mouth on hers. She did not love him; it was so plain, why didn't he see it and feel it and know it? And how could she sleep with him, then, when he came in from the farm, fastidious and separate as she had always been? It was a mystery Kath turned over from time to time in unbelieving astonishment.

Late on those nights when her father came to South Angela, she might wake in the room, usually occupied by a stranger, that adjoined the bathrom she and Mama had to themselves that was kept locked on the stranger's side. She would get up and sit sleepily on the toilet, aware of her father's low voice full of reproach and bitterness, a low, rough monotone. He could have been speaking of money, the source of his usual brooding resentment, or perhaps of Mama's living apart from him. "Lonely," she'd heard him say, and "day after day," and "self-sacrifice." Could he possibly have meant it of himself? But no enlightenment was ever given, for either Elizabeth Rule did not answer or her voice was too low.

Kath sat on the edge of the bed and Elizabeth Rule was in the one easy chair in the room, leaning back, her arms along the arms of the chair and her hands, like two wilted flowers, drooping over the curved ends. "Cordelia Sill came over and told me you and Tissie were in there this afternoon and that you insulted Clayton—that you were rude and forward and sassy. She made it clear you owe him an apology and she was back at her old harping I get so sick of, how difficult it must be to keep a girl like you from becoming impudent."

"But he insulted Tiss! He laughed at her, right in her face, for saying Christmas Science and she was being funny. And all I did was, I asked him how he said r-e-c-e-i-p-t, and he said 'receep,' the way he always does. And I only did it to show him he says his word his way and Tissie says hers hers. So I didn't insult him—"

"Well, the Sills think you did. They're very angry. And that's what matters—"

Kath stared at her in indignation. "Why, it *isn't* what matters. And I won't do it. It isn't fair. If he hadn't insulted Tiss, I'd go. But he did."

Elizabeth Rule got up, tossed off her wrapper, pulled up her petticoat and tied the ribbon of her camisole without saying anything. But after a little, "Then perhaps you'd better get into bed and think it over."

"And no dinner?"

"I expect," said Elizabeth Rule dryly, "that after that club sandwich this afternoon you're probably not very hungry."

"Who told you?"

"Swan did. He said it was just like old times."

At mention of Swan something came clear to Kath. "I see. I'll bet I know who told Mrs. Cordelia Sill we brought those books back for Grant."

Elizabeth Rule stood quite still looking at Kath. "What do you mean?"

"She came out from behind that bead curtain where she'd been listening to everything the way she always does, and she asked Tiss in her special syrupy voice how it feels to have someone like Mrs. Rule bring all those books to your husband. She said nobody ever bothers to bring presents to *her* husband, something so big and heavy that takes all that effort on a hot day, all the way from Columbus. I said I'd helped, but nobody noticed. I'll bet you anything it was Swan told her, though how would Swan know?"

Elizabeth Rule drew on her shirtwaist, buttoned it down the front, then stepped into her skirt and pulled it up and fastened it. "There'd be no reason, I should think," she said presently, "why Grant would tell Swan anything of a personal nature." She seemed to reflect on this. "Though, really, it makes no difference." She went to the bureau, combed and combed her hair, then lifted it up, twisted it in that quick, decisive way she had, and put in the big tortoiseshell pins, her eyes not watching herself in the mirror as they usually did, Kath noticed, but looking off sideways.

Why was she so quiet if it made no difference?

"Don't mind that Mrs. Sill, Mama—don't *mind* her."

Elizabeth Rule turned and walked across to the door and paused there, her hand on the knob. "How could anyone not?"

Kath was reading in bed when there came a knock. "Who is it?"

"It's Grant, Miss Kathy, with your dinner." She heard him chuckle. "Or what you might call your dinner."

"Just a sec—let me put on my robe." She opened the door and there he stood, tall and gravely smiling, impressive in his black suit with the low-cut vest and immaculate starched shirt and black bow tie. As if he had brought a selection of delicacies for the lady of the house, he held a tray with a covered bowl in the center and a smaller one of cut-up fruit at the side.

"So Mama gave in. Do you know why I'm up here, Grant?"

"Oh, yes, Miss Kath, I know."

"Are you on my side?"

He shook his head. "The way I was brought up, young ones never could speak out to their elders."

"So you think I was impudent."

"Well, I think it was up to Tiss to speak up for herself."

Kath took the tray and studied him. "You think I have to apologize?"

"That's between you and your mama."

"If you say it, Grant, then I will."

"No, Miss Kath—you figure it out." And he was about to go when she caught him back.

"Did you like the books, Grant? Were you pleased?"

His face "brighted up," as Tissie would have said. "But didn't your mama tell you?"

"And, Grant, do you think you're going to be what you want to be?"

"Somehow or other, Miss Kath." He paused to consider, becoming grave again. "Somehow or other. The idea's always been there, working away." Then he gave her a quick little smile and a nod and turned and went off down the hall.

Kath put the tray on the bed and closed the door, then slipped off her robe and settled herself with the tray on her lap. Grant, now in his early thirties, had known in his teens what he'd wanted to be. One day he'd been doing yard work for the Buswells and Uncle Tede recalled him saying while he trimmed the front hedge, "I have every intention of pursuing my desire to study the law, Mr. Buswell. I don't know just how I'm to do it, but I intend to search out the means whereby it can be accomplished." Uncle Tede had to laugh. "Can you imagine that young one, a nigger, talking like that, so bookish and high-falutin'—" "Don't say 'nigger,' Tede," interrupted Mama. He was no relative, just a friend, but for some reason she could talk to him like that. "Oh, hell, Elizabeth," he shot back, "I been saying 'nigger' ever since I was born and it's too late to change me now just because you come along and order me to. Anyhow, where was I? Oh, yes— funny he gave up that way of talking. Can't remember just when, but maybe Tiss teased him out of it when they got married. I said to him, 'Well, I declare, Willie Grant. You don't say! Good for you! I don't see you being a lawyer in the near future, but maybe some sort of miracle'll be worked. And it'll have to be *some* miracle, you attaining to the law in this little town. You'll have to get out.' But he never has."

No. He'd met Tissie, then no more than seventeen, when she'd come from Georgia to live with her aunt after her mama and daddy died, and he married her and they stayed where they'd started, in Willowtown. And even though Grant did not speak now as he had in his teens, as long as Kath had known him he'd been wrapped in a kind of unconscious self-possession. You could see he never tried for it; it was just there, in his nature. He always seemed to be turning something over in his mind, always considering something. He wasn't handsome, really, Kath had often thought, and yet because of his tallness and his carriage and his build, he gave that impression. And though he chuckled occasionally at things Kath would say, he rarely laughed outright. Only

Tissie could make him do that: Kath had heard him laugh delightedly during their small private banterings when she visited them out in Willowtown. It seemed to her they had fun together.

She sighed with contentment. There was nothing she loved more than having a meal in bed with her book to read, cozy and quiet, not having to wash and get dressed and go down and mind her manners. She'd pulled back the curtains and put the big windows up as far as they would go on the street side and now a stirring of air was moving among the leaves and there were evening sounds in the streets and she could hear the traveling men closing their doors as, one by one, they went off downstairs to dinner. She could hear the chink of china and silver down there, and sometimes a burst of laughter. Grant would be back now, showing the men to their tables, and the different parties coming in. Everything would be clean and shining and ready. The two waiters, Elliott and Cade (he was new, quick, sassy, cocksure, with a small tense face, very light), would have set the tables with their glossy linen, elaborately folded napkins, and the long-necked glass vases, each with a perfect rose and its leaves in it. Mama and Grant were very particular about that, about the flowers on the two huge blackish sideboards and at the windows and out in the lobby and did all the arranging themselves. Mama would be sitting now at the round family table where only she and Kath and Miss Knowles, the bookkeeper, sat and Ted Morris, the desk clerk, and the two old people who lived in, Mr. Whistler, who was a widower, and Miss Burton, who used to teach at Kath's school, once trim and neat but who'd settled into a kind of bolster shape and got spots down her front which she seemed unaware of.

Kath started on her bread and milk, just nicely between hot and warm, and with just enough butter and a touch of sugar, not too sweet, exactly the way Grant knew she liked it. She picked up *Quentin Durward*, but even though he was in mortal danger she could not concentrate on him. She kept seeing Grant, the way he had of smiling at her in a particular way, as though they had an understanding, so that there was no escape from doing what she knew, as clear as clear, he wanted and expected her to do.

One day up here in the hall—it must have been when she was seven or eight—she'd taken Grant's hand on one side and her mother's on the other and swung them in a flashing moment of pure happiness. She couldn't remember now what they'd been talking about—only that piercing happiness as she skipped between them swinging their hands and laughing. Afterwards she said, "If only Grant wasn't married I would like him for a father. He'd be perfect, wouldn't he?"

She would never forget how Mama stared at her. "Don't ever let me hear you say a thing like that again!"

"But what did I say?" stammered Kath. "Only if he wasn't married—"

"Never speak of it to anyone, do you hear me?" Elizabeth Rule had put her hands on Kath's shoulders and her fingers tightened. "Promise me. Such a thing can so easily be misunderstood no matter how innocently meant."

"But I was only thinking how kind—"

"I know—I know. He *is* kind. But you have no idea how people can take things, how eager they can be to twist them. Remember that, Kath. Remember it."

Of all the innocence, Kath thought, looking back on her child self in amazement.

5  The Road Out

Not until Sunday night did Elizabeth Rule ask Kath if she'd been over to the Sills' to apologize, so that Kath had been happily under the delusion that by the sheerest good luck Mama had forgotten.

"Why haven't you done as I told you?"

"Because Mrs. Sill's gone off to her sister's in Springfield and I thought I'd better wait till she got back."

"What a fib, Kath, when you know perfectly well you'd a million times rather apologize to Clayton alone than to both of them together."

Kath looked down, thinking. "They don't deserve it," she said stubbornly. "We'd be buckling under to that old Cordelia because of those books for Grant and you know we'd be, because I didn't *do* anything."

Mama didn't answer at once, maybe struggling with herself. Then, "You will go over the first thing Tuesday morning, and I will not ask you again."

Kath hadn't been giving Herb a thought, yet when she awoke Monday morning she knew without doubt that she wanted him to come with them to the country. Therefore something inside her, her other self, had been brooding the matter ever since she had last seen him on Friday afternoon, had come to a decision, and settled on this time to announce it.

"Mama?" But Elizabeth Rule, having murmured something, lay unmoving on her back, quite flat and quiet, half waking, half sleeping, Kath knew, in that drifting state of dim, blissful awareness that today was her own and that she need not yet get up though the clock said six. Kath waited. Sometimes when she woke in the early morning needing to go to the bathroom, she held out if Mama were restless, so great was her reluctance to be the cause of another night's broken sleep full of haunting anxieties, endless reflections on the running of the hotel, on a muddled and unhappy life. "Yes, Kath?" she said half an hour later, as if no time at all had passed.

"Mama, I thought I'd like Herb to come."

Silence. "But not out of some sort of consideration—"

"Why, no! Just because I want him. Do I have to have a reason? Do you mind?"

Another silence. "I don't understand you. Why have you changed?"

"But changed from what? He's my friend."

However, Chattie wouldn't have it. Her long oval face turned sulky and her chin and mouth took on their heavy look. The two of them, she and Kath, were outside the stable at the back of the Jameson house and Chattie was already in the pony cart, impatiently ready to be away while Elizabeth Rule and Margaret Jameson were going on and on about unimportant nothings up on the back porch; Margaret Jameson didn't feel well and wasn't coming—there was some sort of private explanation.

Kath had been talking to Little Plum, pressing her face against his silky neck and breathing in his rich, warm, horsey smell. He had been named Little Plum by Kath the minute she ran over to him that first afternoon Mr. Jameson had brought him home two weeks ago, not only because he was so firm and fat but most of all because he was exactly the color—brown with a purplish sheen to his coat—of a certain kind of plum she remembered that revealed a golden flesh when you bit into it. "Little Plum, Little Plum," and she had put her arms around his neck, rubbing her cheek against him with deep, sensuous pleasure, and he had turned his head and snuffled her neck and she had looked directly into his liquid brown-gold eye. So Little Plum he had remained, and oddly enough Chattie made no fuss even though he was her pony and she was very possessive about what was hers and usually rejected Kath's suggestions about anything.

"I don't want Herb," Chattie said now. Then suddenly she flared up, "Just because he's stuck on you—it makes me sick!"

Kath shrugged. "All right, then," she said indifferently. "Stay home. Mama'n I'll get someone else to take us out." She knew Chattie to the core and turned her face away to hide her smile. Chattie had been talking of nothing but a picnic in the country, in the orchard, for the past week, and ten minutes later when Mama and Kath arrived at Herb's house, they were in the pony cart with Chattie, who had the reins in her hands. It would be her first long journey and she wouldn't have missed it for anything, this chance to drive Little Plum six miles out of South Angela and back again in the evening, even though, as she said on the way over to Herb's, "Now we know the truth about Kath—who's her best friend, but i-*ma*-gine!" in pure disgust.

To which Elizabeth Rule replied unexpectedly, "No, Chattie, I don't think we do—not the whole truth. Not you or anybody else." Nor did Kath, and she did not trouble to question. "Hurry now, dear," Mama said when Chattie drew up outside the green house. "The heat's getting up. Don't stay in there forever." It was by now eight o'clock.

At first, in the Mayhews' tiny kitchen, Kath thought perhaps everything might be all right, even though Mrs. Mayhew was talking again about that fence out in front she wanted Herb to fix. There was no sense, she said, in his deliberately neglecting it day after day the state it was in.

"But couldn't he do it tomorrow, Mrs. Mayhew? I'll help him. If you let him go, I'll come over tomorrow and help. It'd be fun."

"*Fun!*" retorted Mrs. Mayhew in derision. "*Fun!* That's no play job." She was a little, thin, dried-up woman, bitterly resentful of all that had happened since her husband died right after Herb was born in her forties and left her everything to manage and nothing to manage on. Her eyes narrowed and she took in Kath's face as if to get to the bottom of something. "What on earth're you so blamed anxious for him to go for? What's all the fuss about?"

Kath gazed at her in bewilderment. She had always avoided Herb's mother whenever possible and wasn't used to coming to grips with her about anything. "But why shouldn't we ask him? We thought he'd—"

"You thought he'd *what?*" Mrs. Mayhew interrupted, high up and coming down hard on the last word. "Enjoy himself?" she said acidly. "Not *you wanted* him, but you thought he'd enjoy himself. Very kind!" She seemed in a state of pent-up agitation, a kind of sizzling, irritated nervousness.

And now all at once her eyes shifted from Kath's face and looked beyond, and Kath turned and there was Herb standing in the doorway. She'd been aware of him walking back and forth overhead, aware of something ominous in that sound; she'd heard a door slam, the cover of the wooden chest that stood at the foot of his bed bang down and, just now, his feet racketing on the naked stairs. There he stood, motionless, as if carved, his eyes staring straight at his mother, never wavering for an instant, as if he were completely unaware of

Kath's presence. And his face—*his face*. She had never seen him like this in all the years she had known him. He seemed consumed by anger, by a white and frozen fury, and his silver eyes were terrible in their intensity: luminous, as if they shone, fueled by some inner conflagration.

"Where are my things?" he said in a low, even voice. "Where are they? What have you done with them?"

"*What* things—"

"You know what things," he breathed. "*You know.* My fossils. My rocks. My books." His hands worked; his whole body was fiercely, threateningly alive, and yet he never moved from the doorway. "You've cleaned my room. Where are my things? What have you done with my books?"

Kath, who couldn't take her gaze from Herb, was aware of Mrs. Mayhew's quickened breathing. "What d'you mean, your *books!* All that baby stuff. I never touched the others—the ones that are fit for a boy your age. You're a great grown thing, and I gave all that other stuff to the Ladies Aid, where it belongs. You're past all that, Herb Mayhew, an' you know it. I'd be ashamed," she shrilled suddenly, "to be keeping books other children could use, little children, *The Brownies* an' *The Secret Garden* an' all those castle an' magic an' fairy tale books—"

Herb didn't answer at once, and then he said very low and cold, "Uncle Bob sent me those from England, my Nesbit and Andrew Lang books. I want them back. They're mine—*my* books and *my* fossils and *my* rocks. How dare you throw out what's mine—and without even asking me when I told you never to go in my room and touch my things again. I want them all back—"

"Well, you'll not have them!" cried Mrs. Mayhew, and as Herb moved forward a step, she got in behind the kitchen table—Kath heard the scrape of it and turned and saw Mrs. Mayhew's white face and blazing eyes. "This is my house, an' I intend to keep it clean, an' I will not have your trash—all that fossil an' rock dirt sifted all over the floor up there and rubbish squirreled away in the closet. I will *not*." She drew breath for a second. "What d'you want to keep those little kids' books for, anyhow?" she demanded.

"For my children. Just because I don't read them anymore—or hardly ever—doesn't mean I haven't a right to keep what's mine. They're for my children."

Mrs. Mayhew's jaw dropped, something Kath had read of but had never actually seen. Now there was a small throbbing silence, and then, finally, "Your *chil*dren!" The words were scarcely audible, but though Kath could never afterwards have described the exact tone of Mrs. Mayhew's voice, she would never forget it nor ever fail to be able to reproduce it precisely in her own mind. "Your *chil*dren!" the little woman repeated as if Herb had told her of animals that could speak or of walking trees. "O-oh, my honey!" and all at once she came from behind the table and held her arms out and started toward him as though she were going to enfold him in an embrace that would protect him forever from all the wretchedness life was holding in store for him. He watched her coming with a look of utter horror and, just as she reached him, brutally struck aside her outstretched hands and plunged across the kitchen, wrenched open the screen door and ran down the steps. Mrs. Mayhew darted after him, through the door and out into the yard. "It's no use," she bawled. "Where're you going, Herb Mayhew! You come *back* here—they're *gone*—" and she stood for a moment, watching him run off along the street. Then she turned and came in, and she had one hand up to her mouth, and when she got inside she stood there, staring at nothing. "Fairy tales," she said, but not to Kath. She had forgotten Kath. "A big fellow his age reading fairy tales—staying off by himself and reading what isn't true because he can't stand what *is*." She shook her head and kept on shaking it as if she might be going on indefinitely. "Nobody knows what it's like—an' he wanted them for his children. My God! That's what I mean. How's a person to make him see—make him understand?" She stood thinking, as though over her own question, then all at once came to and looked up and saw Kath. And she must have read the expression on Kath's face and in her eyes. "You don't fool me for one minute, Kathryn Rule," she said, her voice hardening. "Not for one minute. But just let me tell you something. You an' your ma don't have to be thoughtful about Herb. I know her—you're growing up just like her, an' my boy don't need anything done out o' kindness—"

"But it *wasn't* out of kindness, Mrs. Mayhew—" Kath's voice shook and her face abominably blushed. She could feel the slow stain spreading. "Why can't you just—"

"You get on out o' here," Mrs. Mayhew said fiercely. "Get right on out an' don't come back. An' you mind your own business. You an' your ma." And she went to the screen and held it open until Kath got outside.

Elizabeth Rule had stepped down from the pony cart and was coming along the front path when Kath rounded the corner of the house. "Kath—what is it?" She stood and took in the look on Kath's face. "What made Mrs. Mayhew shout after Herb like that? What did she mean it wouldn't be any use? What wouldn't be any use?"

"Trying to get his things back from the Ladies Aid—"

"What things?"

"She's given them away without even asking him—his books, his fairy tales and the Nesbit books and all his rocks and fossils. She was raving at him about clearing up his dirt, and then all at once when he said he wanted those books for his children, she put her arms out and called him 'my honey' in that sickening voice— 'Oh, my *honey!*' she said, and I could have killed her. I'll never go back. She doesn't need to worry about that. She says we're to mind our own business, you and me, and that we don't need to be kind."

By this time Kath and Elizabeth Rule were back at the pony cart, and Kath was climbing up behind Chattie when Chattie said smartly, "Well, and weren't you being? Why on earth else *would* you invite him?"

"You shut up!" shouted Kath in a blaze. "I did not invite Herb out of kindness. I invited him because he's my friend, and why don't *you* try minding your own business?" She was aware of her breath coming the way Mrs. Mayhew's had in the kitchen when she was defending herself against Herb—fast and hard.

"That will do, Kath." Elizabeth Rule paused to look at her before getting up in the cart. "If we're to have any sort of—"

But Chattie had her chin up. "Maybe I don't *want* to go on this trip today. Maybe I don't *like* being told to shut up—"

"Chattie," said Mama, and she got up beside her and arranged her skirts, "Herb is Kath's friend whether you like him or not. As for driving out to the country, if you don't want to go, then turn around and drive back. Nobody's stopping you."

Chattie sat for a moment, her back straight and the tilt of her head offended, and Kath knew exactly the way her underlip would be pushed out and the way her chin would look. But all at once Chattie clucked to Little Plum and gave the reins a flick along his back, and by the time they had got out to where Willowtown started, she was in the highest spirits, laughing and telling Elizabeth Rule something funny Dillis their housekeeper had said, immensely set up, no doubt, Kath thought, by the number of heads turned, especially out in Willowtown, to watch them spanking by in the smart new wicker pony cart with its black and red rubber tired wheels twinkling silently along the clay road, and Little Plum, with his round haunches glistening in the sun, his thick main and tail swaying out and his small hooves making a quick velvety *thock*-thock, *thock*-thock, *thock*-thock in the deep yellow dust. To Kath this was the sound of a summer day in the country, and there was the wicker hamper at her feet that Swan had packed for them under Grant's guidance, and Aunt Lily would have made Mama a birthday cake.

They drew up outside Tiss's garden and here she came past the hollyhocks, all decked out in a new dress of lavender-and-green plaid poplin with a frill of fine pleating standing up around her neck so that her face was made to look like a dark gold flower, and the pleating tilted over at her throat and rippled in a froth down her bosom. She had a bag with her work clothes in it, for she fully intended to make a refined appearance riding out through the rest of Willowtown. She would no more have thought of riding out in her work clothes than going naked, though over them she would wear a voluminous starched apron. Tiss had a genius for dressmaking that made Aunt Hattie and Aunt Maud Buswell's efforts look clumsy and amateurish, but Tiss found sewing tedious for anyone but herself. However, if she'd had the patience she would no doubt have got a devilish pleasure in seeing how many of the Buswells' customers she could have captured. "Plenty!" Mama said, who herself always managed to tease Tiss into making something for her, just as Tiss had now the habit of getting rainwater to wash Mama's hair, which she afterwards fanned dry, lifting and fanning, lifting and fanning, with slow, rhythmical movements of her slim wrists and long fingers that Kath loved to watch, that soothed her to watch. Kath had an idea that Tiss would have done anything for Mama.

"Good morning, Mizz Rule—Miss Chattie—Buttonbox!" sang out Tiss. "Ain't it a gra-a-and day?" She opened the back of the cart and let down the steps and swept up, lifting her skirt with a gesture of exaggerated refinement, chuckled at herself as she sat down opposite Kath, and joined in the chattering and laughter as they got out into the countryside.

But Kath was hearing another voice. "And why *did* you want me to go?" It was as if Herb were sitting there opposite her instead of Tiss. Tell me the truth—*tell me the truth.* She twisted away, twisted sideways. You always had to tell him the truth; he was too serious. He was tiresome he was so serious. Now he would be at the Ladies Aid, and had he got his books back and found the fossils broken and scattered that his mother had probably tossed over the back fence into an empty lot? Mrs. Mayhew would never begin to guess at the depths of rage she could make boil inside her own son. But Kath knew. She knew things about Herb Mrs. Mayhew would never know. As for the terrible meaning of his mother's dripping, "Oh, my *honey!*" she would never forget that moment when Herb had struck aside the outstretched hands with one furious blow.

They bowled along yellow roads shaded by elms and maples and locusts that bordered the rich rolling meadowlands and vast fields of timothy and corn. You could smell fennel and the wild sweet clover that grew waist high in the ditches where bees hummed and where rabbits and chipmunks were hiding. Sometimes they darted out and scudded across the road. Bobolinks were sending up their clear cries from the fields of timothy; thrushes rustled in the hedgerows, and every now and then a meadowlark called. This, to Kath, was the most beautiful sound of any: a clear, liquid burbling like water running over stones. No—not that—not that! It was indescribable.

After a little more than half an hour they came to the midpoint of their journey. As they approached a watering trough under a stand of mossy willows just where the main road turned, crossed the railroad tracks, and sent off a narrow meandering side road that led to Uncle Paul's, a rabbit scuttered suddenly under Little Plum's hooves. He stopped abruptly, whinnying with fright, reared up between his shafts, and tilted the pony cart backwards. Chattie squealed, Elizabeth Rule's big straw hat was jolted over her eyes, and Tiss rose up and was somehow out of the cart in an instant and running around to Little Plum, who had subsided and was standing quiet and trembling. Mama started to laugh, seeming unable to stop herself, while she settled her hat again. And Kath hopped down and together she and Tiss led Little Plum to the trough where he plunged his soft nose deep into the green water, slobbering and sucking up the delicious coolness. While he sucked and gurgled and blew out his soft lips, tossed up his head and plunged his nose into the water again, Kath reached out for handfuls of ripe blackberries, still warm from the morning sun, and when she pressed them into her greedy mouth, their intoxicating fragrance mingled with their wild deep flavor so that she could scarcely tell where fragrance left off and taste began. Tiss reached out too, and they watched each other with bright eyes over their cupped hands spilling in the berries just as though they were the same age.

All along the road to Uncle Paul's the ancient rail fences were chained to the earth by this thicket of blackberry vines and by a tangled jungle of bracken and hawthorne and elderberry. Day after day now, Aunt Lily would be making blackberry jam and elderberry wine and jelly, and storing away hazelnuts.

"Tiss—Kath!" Elizabeth Rule cried all at once. "You get back in here—you won't have a bit of appetite left for this enormous lunch Swan fixed for us. Tiss, if you drip blackberry juice on that dress of yours, it will be a positive crime. It'll never come out. Come on, now, wash your faces and get back in."

"I want some too," said Chattie, offended at being left out

of the fun, and started to climb down, but Mama caught her back. Unaccountably, as she often did such things, Tiss suddenly lifted her long arms, wound them together, tilted her head, pursued her tulip lips, and let out a thin thread of song.

"Oh-h-h, my beau-u-tiful dress," she crooned, swaying, spiraling slowly, her eyes closed. "My beau-u-tiful, beau-u-tiful dress!" Then she and Kath washed their hands in the trough, laughing together as over some private joke, rinsed off their mouths, wiped them dry on Tiss's handkerchief, and got back into the cart.

"They're silly," said Chattie in a disgusted grown-up voice. "I've never seen such silliness."

6 🌿 A Lake of Meadowlarks

It was always the dogs who greeted visitors first, having got the reverberations of hoofbeats through the earth, no doubt. They went wild—Old Fred, who was almost blind, and Orlo and Dusty and little Pippy—barking as if they'd lost their minds, flinging themselves along the road, then taking the pony cart the last lap, leaping in a frenzy in front and behind and on either side. And so Aunt Lily would already be standing there on the wide, cool, vine-covered veranda with Pillow, her big black-and-white cat with the snowy patch on his chest, sitting gravely at her feet. Aunt Lily was as pretty now as when she'd been a girl, Elizabeth Rule always said, and she would run down and hug Mama as if they'd been apart for years, and then Uncle Paul would come somberly and unharness the horses of whoever had brought Mama and Kath.

He came now and got busy with Little Plum, not saying much, but then he never did; always keeping occupied, Kath thought, so he wouldn't have to. And it came to her mind how he would stand up at the table, handsome as a god, to say grace in stern, reproving tones, as if admonishing whoever was gathered at his board that they would fail to be thankful for this, his bounty, to their shame. And when he led Little Plum over to the pasture, leaving the cart under the Norway spruce, Little Plum galloped madly away, around and around the pasture, then got down and rolled as if he could never have enough, and for the first time Uncle Paul smiled. He stood there quite silent, smiling to himself, his hands in his back pockets, watching Little Plum in his ecstasy. Then he turned and looked at Mama.

"I'd like to speak to you before you go this afternoon, Elizabeth." Chattie was up on the fence, laughing at the antics of her pony, and Tissie and Aunt Lily were talking about what had to be done and where it would be best to start. Elizabeth Rule looked up at him.

"Really, Paul? Why not now?"

"This afternoon will do soon enough."

"Will it, then!" she said, and with a lift of the eyebrows slid her arm through Kath's and turned away.

At noon, Tiss and Aunt Lily and Mama came out to the little grassy orchard where they were to have their picnic, and Aunt Lily flung out a clean old tablecloth and tossed pillows around. Tiss had the big wicker basket and Mama the jugs of coffee and milk and a bottle of cream.

All morning, while Elizabeth Rule lay on a canvas deck chair in the shade of the garden with a magazine in her lap which she occasionally lifted and then let fall again, Kath and Chattie had been exploring in almost the same absorbed ecstasy that had overwhelmed Little Plum in the pasture. This was Chattie's first visit to the farm, though Kath had asked her before, but Chattie had seemed to have in mind some dirty little place, and Kath would never have imagined how Chattie could be changed, her whole face illumined with expectation and eagerness for the next surprise. Chattie was—incredibly—engrossed in something outside herself for the only time Kath could remember.

Elizabeth Rule stretched out on the grass. "I'm so tired,

Lily," she said. "I can't seem to get rid of my tiredness." She lay looking up through the boughs of the stunted, worm-eaten old apple trees, hollowed by flickers and woodpeckers, that had been planted here, Aunt Lily had once told Kath, by Johnny Appleseed sixty years or more ago when all this land was wild.

Mama had folded her hands in her lap and closed her eyes when she wished on her birthlay candles, and a curious little smile hovered around her lips while she made her secret wish. "What did you wish, Mama—what was it?" But Elizabeth Rule only smiled to herself, and Kath never said that she had added her own, just on the off chance. "Please God," she had prayed with passionate intensity, "please let Mama and me go and live in the Green Mountains with Grandmother," even as she knew underneath how hopeless was her plea to a remote and unimaginable God.

A little later, "What is it Paul wants to talk to me about, Lily?" Kath heard, while Tiss and Chattie were joking about something, whereupon Kath stilled inside and turned her attention to catch Aunt Lily's answer. But Aunt Lily wasn't sure. "I think something to do with Grant," she said, very low.

Kath looked and saw Mama's glance waver sideways, then back to Aunt Lily's face. "But what?" Aunt Lily shook her head, and Kath knew that Mama knew what it was Uncle Paul had it in mind to speak of. But Kath herself could not imagine. Now Mama's eyes were closed and Kath saw that she had fallen asleep as suddenly and completely as though her weariness had drowned her. She was on her back and Aunt Lily curled down beside her, and with a hand on Mama's arm she too went to sleep.

Silently Tiss rose, unfolding herself like a leggy bird, held out her hands to the girls, and they went off into the woods.

There were rustlings in the underbrush at their approach, perhaps rabbits or pheasants, but no bird spoke in the thick heat. Here in the enclosed woods the smell of growing things was intense, the smell of trees, oak and beech and maple and wild cherry, of ferns and fennel and fungus, pennyroyal and elder. All was quiet except for a faint trickling and the constant hum of woodflies dancing over their heads, their minute wings sending out a sudden glitter whenever a cluster of them moved through a sword of green light. Kath squatted down at the brook that flowed into the spring house and plunged her hands into the water after sunfish and silversides that darted through her fingers, flashing into bronze sunny spots and out again.

"There's a pool farther on where Aunt Lily and I used to swim naked. It was delicious, but she must have told Uncle Paul because we never do it anymore."

They came out on the far side onto a rise that swept down into a small cupped valley in the midst of hills deserted and silent as though freshly created, never pressed by the foot of man. The descent was gradual and irregular, full of hidden hollows, and as the three of them moved forward, they became aware of a continuous, liquid murmuration, filled with such bubbling sweetness that something turned inside of Kath to hear it. "Tiss, what can it be!" But Tiss pressed her hand to silence her and she made the girls kneel and wait before they took another step, and presently, when they had inched forward a little, they could look over into the next hollow where they beheld a lake of meadowlarks.

The gray-gold gathering was in constant motion, birds fluttering up and sinking again, flying off and returning while, without cease, the clear bubbling talk rose and fell, questioning, answering, never very loud, though sometimes a lancet note, like the beginning of one bird's song, pierced through but never finished, as though this were not the time for song but only the quiet, intimate communion of these hundreds of kindred spirits.

At last Tiss motioned the girls back, and they withdrew from their watching place and got themselves up into the woods again without once disturbing that subdued symphony. She stood for a moment with her hands pressed to her lips. "There is something a person could keep inside herself for the rest of her life."

"But *what?*" pressed Chattie. "What do you mean, Tiss? What exactly could a person keep inside?"

Tiss considered Chattie, her large eyes leisurely taking in Chattie's face. "Child," she said presently, "if I have to explain it wouldn't really be any use my telling."

About four that afternoon, Elizabeth Rule, lazy and content after her long, deep nap in the orchard, stretched her arms out on the dining room table where they were all having tea. Uncle Paul had come in too and was having coffee. Mama had her cup in her hands, twisting it now this way, now that, trying to determine her future, and Tiss leaned over her shoulder.

"You'll go on a long journey, Mizz Rule, that's one thing certain. See there now, how that line goes on an' on—that's what I mean, an' just two people, you an' Miss Button."

"Maybe to the mountains, Mama—to the Green Mountains!"

But Elizabeth Rule was paying no attention. She was looking at Aunt Lily with that private, shining, teasing gaiety that always came into her eyes when she and Aunt Lily could remember something that nobody else knew anything about. "We went on a long journey once, didn't we, Lily? Mother and Dad and you and me, down to Cuba, and the storm came up on Nepe Bay and everybody was sick, but not I, for some incredible reason, and there was that enormously rich Cuban who wanted to marry me. Oh, Lily—remember when he—when he—" But she couldn't finish, for the two of them, infuriatingly, had gone off into peels of laughter and Uncle Paul's expression never changed so that you could tell he felt excluded, unnecessary, and therefore insulted.

"When he *what*, Mama—tell us, tell us!"

> *"Put on your camisola,*
> *Jump into my gondola*
> *And bunkydoodle-i-do with me,"*

sang Aunt Lily.

Elizabeth Rule had to wipe her eyes. "You were a wicked little devil, Lily. You egged him on, making him think I was interested, just to find out what he'd—"

"But he was the handsomest thing I'd ever seen. You should have married him, Liz. So considerate and mannerly—the most exquisite manners. You'd have been wrapped in luxury, but, no—you had to go and—"

"Lily!"

"Just think, Kath," and Aunt Lily turned her gray-blue gaze on Kath, making it brilliant and piercing as though trying to see her differently, "you might have been a deep golden brown with long black hair and *black,* glittering eyes and an even fierier spirit than you have now. I doubt we could have stood you—"

"Well *I* couldn't have," said Chattie, "and that's a fact."

"But am I fiery?" asked Kath in surprise, trying to remember herself. "I don't think I am. Mama's the one—"

"Oh, *is* she, now!" exclaimed Elizabeth Rule, tremors of amusement still playing over her lips.

"Which reminds me," said Uncle Paul, cutting abruptly, with obvious impatience, across this foolish feminine chatter, "have you apologized to Clayton Sill yet, Kathryn?" Kath stared at him, knowing perfectly well he hadn't been reminded at all, but had had the matter of Clayton on his mind ever since he had been told—by the Sills themselves, it must have been—what she had said.

There was a small tight silence in which the lightheartedness of the moment became rigid with expectancy and unease. Kath was aware that the cup had ceased turning in Mama's hands, though she still appeared to be studying it. But Aunt Lily had straightened.

"Oh, Paul," she said deprecatingly, "perhaps—"

"I think," said Elizabeth Rule, "there's no need to trouble, Paul. I will handle it."

All at once Aunt Lily scraped back her chair and began taking plates off the table, and Tiss moved in behind. "Come on, Chattie," said Aunt Lily. "How about getting the plates on your side." Chattie never budged, and Mama's head turned, and she regarded Chattie, and Chattie rose as though pulled by strings.

When they had gone, Uncle Paul leaned forward. "And it isn't just that—Kath's behavior. That's the least of it. I will not have Clayton Sill or anyone else in South Angela talking around town about my family—"

"I don't know what you mean," said Elizabeth Rule, and Kath recognized the dangerous curl within the deceptive lightness of her tone. An implacable power was contained there and behind the ivory pallor of her face. The help at the hotel knew that tone, and Uncle Paul knew it, but he was as implacable as Mama.

"I think perhaps you do, Elizabeth. Clayton Sill tells me you actually *bought* Grant some law books, six volumes! And that you brought them all the way from Columbus. I told him I didn't believe it but he said I'd only to ask you. Do you think everybody doesn't know how little Boughtridge pays you, and that you have a husband out on a little two-bit farm somewhere? And to think that for a *black* man—" Kath thought she'd never seen Uncle Paul so angry, not even the time when she'd been seven and had mindlessly, in front of two or three of the hired hands, out of pure high spirits, given him a great hard whack on the behind which must really have hurt as well as startled and humiliated him, because he'd twisted round, caught her across his knee, pulled up her dress, and given her the smacking of her life. Now Elizabeth Rule put her cup down so suddenly that it chattered on the saucer, then laced her fingers together, and Kath saw that her knuckles were white.

"I love my sister," she said in an unhurried voice. "But what I do with my life I do according to my own lights and convictions, according to what I think is right and not what you or anybody else thinks. I feel under no obligation to explain any of my actions to you, but for Lily's sake I will. I got those books from my friend Maizie Hammond. They were books her son used in law school and doesn't need any longer. Grant couldn't afford to buy them new and he's been hunting for a good used set, so I couldn't see why he shouldn't have them for the little effort it took Kath and me to bring them back on the train. Now if you feel you have to explain anything of a private nature to the people of South Angela or take any of their needling about something that doesn't concern them, that's up to you. But as I see it, what I do is my affair and none of anyone else's."

With this, Elizabeth Rule got up and turned and walked out into the kitchen and Kath did not know if she could possibly look at Uncle Paul, much as she longed to. After a little, she forced herself and it seemed to her that his nose had been sharpened as if by a knife. It had gone completely white—it stood out like a beak. Now all at once, he too got up—so suddenly that his chair toppled and he went out of the door and along the hall and the screen door banged. They would not see him again, she thought, before she and Chattie and Mama and Tiss left; in fact, she felt it quite likely she might never see him again.

How could they ever come back to the farm now—it would be impossible. And it was sad when this had been one of the happiest of days, happy because she'd been able to show the farm, which she had always particularly loved, to Chattie—all the special places: the buttery at the top of the cellar stairs, cool and dark and smelling of cookies and pies, of maple sugar and apples and spices and raisins and cider, a subtle, delectable mingling of all of them together; and then the barn with its cathedral-like emptiness high up under the gambrel roof above the hay where, in the lofty shadows, birds flew around and around, calling in plaintive tones until they escaped, while down below, the enormous workhorses pulled hay from their feed racks, blew lustily through their nostrils and stamped and stamped their huge hairy hooves; then the pasture where Kath and Chattie, clutching dark green bouquets of kale, got up on the fence and Kath called out to Mollie, standing in the big herd of Guernseys and Jerseys in the shade of a grove of oaks, "Come on, Mollie, *come* on, you old lazy girl, you! Now you watch, Chattie," and the whole herd lifted their heads, the heads turned, and all those somber, questioning gazes, the big brown eyes with feminine shadows underneath, centered upon the waving figures—what was wanted of them? they seemed to ask in gentle bewilderment—but presently a single cow separated herself from the general mass and began moving toward Kath, who shook her bouquet and called urgently, "Come on, Mollie, *come on,* you old slowpoke. Don't you remember me? Come *on,* come *on!*" and gradually, very gradually, Mollie began to gather speed, to canter, you might say, swaying from end to end like a lumbering ship in heavy seas, her great udder swinging, and Chattie, beside herself with excitement, was yelling, "Let *me*, Kath—let *me!*" until, at once terrified and fascinated, she could feed the kale into that pink maw, edged with big yellow teeth, that breathed out its heavy breath, "—and after that," Chattie had remembered contentedly, finishing off a wedge of birthday cake at the end of the picnic, "we went to the chicken yard and sat down under a tree and let the little chicks run all over our laps, and some of them stayed there and went to sleep and I could pick them up in my hands and hold them and stroke them and it was all quiet and peaceful and lazy, and then we took some of the older ones that had mud balls on their toes and knocked the mud balls off. Kath says the next time we come maybe we could candle eggs. Could we, Aunt Lily? Would you let me?" so that clearly it had been in Chattie's mind that whenever Kath came to the farm after this, she, Chattie, would come too; you could see that she had been taking it for granted.

Kath was pushing crumbs around in her lap, gathering them into a little heap, when someone came in and slid a hand along her shoulders, and Kath knew by the fragrance that it was Aunt Lily. "I'm so sorry, Kath," she said. "I'm so very sorry," but Kath could not reply.

How can you love him, she wanted to demand, and was filled with a hard and bitter rebellion against men like Uncle Paul, like her own father, who expected to be able to direct their women's affairs according to their own light and word without discussion, nor any least possibility of it. *You do as I say.* How can you love him? but would never have asked it, aware that inexplicably Aunt Lily adored her husband—yes, that was the word, in spite of his severity, his hardness—and knew too that Uncle Paul would have done "anything within reason" (she had heard it put that way) for his pretty wife. Something existed between those two, something intensely private that one never saw any obvious sign of, except possibly a word now and then or some slight gesture caught out of the corner of one's eye, something that Kath thought she would never be able to understand considering the nature of Uncle Paul.

One of the men had come and harnessed Little Plum, and now Chattie was up in the front seat ready to be off. Aunt Lily and Tiss and Mama were coming down the front steps into the long shadows of late afternoon lying across the grass. Kath went to them to kiss Aunt Lily good-bye, while Tiss crossed to the cart with the picnic basket. Mama and Aunt Lily, murmuring together, paused where they stood and turned to each other, and Pillow wove himself back and forth against their legs as if he knew the visit had come to an end. Now the two put their arms around each other, then Mama drew back and brushed her fingers gently against Aunt Lily's cheek.

"I'll not be coming again, Lily," she said. "You understand—"

"Oh, Liz—he thought you'd *bought* them. He misunderstood 'bought' for 'brought.' Please, Liz, don't resent him. He was only thinking of what was—"

"But I know he wouldn't want to see me again. I always rub him the wrong way, the kind of woman I am, the things I do, the things I say. And I never take his advice. But we'll see each other, Lily. You'll come into town?"

Aunt Lily took Mama's hand in both her own. "Nobody," she said, "could keep me from seeing my own sister. Because that wouldn't be right."

And so they were ready to go, but it seemed Chattie had arrived at a decision. She wanted Elizabeth Rule to drive Little Plum back.

"Oh, let me, Chattie—let me!" cried Kath. She hadn't let

on, but her envy of Chattie's being in charge of Little Plum had been deep and sharp all the way out.

"No," said Chattie, "I don't trust him. I want it to be a grown-up."

"Could I, Miss Chattie?" said Tiss unexpectedly. "I've been behind many a horse in my time. I don't think Little Plum'd act up with me. Would you mind, Mizz Rule?"

"But I want to sit up front all the same," said Chattie. And so Tiss got up in Chattie's place, and Chattie moved over and Mama got in back with Kath. And off they went, the dogs leaping about in their usual frenzy, and as long as they could keep Aunt Lily in view she stood waving good-bye and sending them kisses. She had Pillow on one arm, his plumy tail draped over and his front paws resting on her shoulder.

"Poor old Pillow," said Mama, for he was an eerie, unpredictable cat, whom you could not safely pick up nor take into your lap, for he might stiffen suddenly and from being a perfectly amenable family animal, look up at you with bright feral eyes, whereupon you knew instantly that he was about to bite. He loved only Aunt Lily, of all human beings, and allowed her to do with him exactly as she pleased.

"If we should have a child," Uncle Paul had said, "he will have to be done away with."

"But he's my cat, Paul—you couldn't do that. He'll feel toward the baby as he does me."

"I wouldn't trust him."

However, it did not seem as if Aunt Lily would ever have a child, and there was all that spacious old house to fill.

Kath heard the whistle of the train that drew into South Angela somewhere around five-thirty every evening. And again she was overcome—perhaps because of the melancholy in that long drawn-out warning rolling across the quiet land—

by the thought of having lost the farm and the animals, the dogs and Mollie and the workhorses on whose back she had so often ridden, and being able to help Aunt Lily make jellies and preserves and pies, and slice apples and fry them in butter for breakfast, and get things from the buttery, climb the crooked apple trees and eat the little sweet-sour windfalls filled to dripping with juice, or go off exploring with Aunt Lily and the dogs into the woods and hills, or just the dogs if Aunt Lily were too busy to come.

Suddenly she thought of Tiss standing at the edge of the woods with her hands to her lips, and how she had said that *that*, the experience of the meadowlarks, was something to keep for the rest of their lives. But something underneath the thought oppressed her, something said during the afternoon. Yes—it had been Tiss. They were coming back through the woods and Kath had pulled them from the path to show them the pool she and Aunt Lily had used to swim in, and as they stood there Kath had said, "Listen—how still it is," and so it was, until the cicadas started up a buzzing in the trees.

"*Still*ness!" said Tiss. "There's something I don't need, I can tell you. It's all I get now when Grant's home—him and his law books. Not so sure I thank you for that, Miss Button. Not so sure. Me and Grant, we used to have the most fun, but seems like those old black books got him by the nose. He's gone a long way off, an' if we talk, I always feel his mind's on somethin' else—not on me."

Well, but Tiss would have to learn about a person studying, about wanting to study. If Grant had ambition—again the train sent forth its warning whistle, only nearer now, much nearer, and Kath, who had suddenly been jerked upright, raised her head. Nobody had said a word, yet all at once a dart of terror shot through her. Little Plum had broken into a mad, flat-out gallop and she saw that, without her being aware of it, they had come onto the main road and were approaching the crossing where the road curved over the railroad tracks. The train was coming toward them on their right and Little Plum, his ears laid back and neck straining forward, was racing with insane determination toward that meeting point of track and road.

Chattie began to shriek, a single, sustained, high-pitched note. Kath saw her swaying backward toward the side of the cart and thought how at any moment she might be thrown out, while in the same instant Elizabeth Rule, who was sitting behind Tiss, got up in her seat, leaned forward against Tiss with her arms around her, and took hold of the reins, gripping them just above Tiss's grip.

"Get Chattie, Kath—" and Kath, staying tight where she was in order to give herself anchorage, leaned forward and put her arms around Chattie's swaying body.

Little Plum was out of his mind. Perhaps he had never suffered that piercing whistle directly in his ears; perhaps, even, he had never been close to a train. The looming monstrous shape, with its brutal swiftness and racket, the apparent inevitability of their meeting, together with the unceasing shriek that was issuing from Chattie, and Elizabeth Rule's desperate cries to Little Plum, combined to make this whole thing something Kath could not credit. At any moment she would wake. But she did not wake. And the train and Little Plum and the cart were drawing together—when finally, under the inexorable tug of both Tiss's and Elizabeth Rule's hands, he suddenly tossed back his head and in that instant they got the better of him. He reared up on his hind legs, then dropped abruptly and swerved alongside the train thundering past not five feet from them, and Tiss and Mama dragged his head round and headed him away into a roadside ditch where he came to a trembling halt, unable to go ahead or to maneuver sideways because of the fence in front of him.

As the Pullman cars and then the baggage sped past, the four of them sat there in silence trying to compose themselves, to realize just what had happened, but Chattie had begun to sob, leaning against Tiss, and Tiss neither moved nor spoke but sat there with her knees apart and the reins hanging loosely from her hands.

Now the train was gone and Kath jumped down and went round to Little Plum, who was still trembling, his eyes starting from their sockets, the whites wildly showing. He jerked his head, and as it came up, she saw the blood on his mouth flecked with foam. "My Little Plum—my little horse—" and she put her arms around him and pressed her face into his soaking neck, and it seemed to her she could feel his heart sending its thundering beat along the arteries. She took his face between her hands, speaking to him and putting her cheek against his. Somehow, for what reason she could not have explained, she loved him in this instant more than ever. She would have given anything to have owned him.

Now Elizabeth Rule called to her saying they were going to back him up and get him out of the ditch, and obediently, quietly, with his head down, he allowed Kath to lead him up onto the road.

But still Tiss did not move. "The train—" she said. "The train—" The reins lay slack in her fingers and she was staring straight ahead, her gaze fixed. Kath laid a hand on her arm and shook it. "Tiss?" she said, and Tissie slowly brought her gaze round to rest on Kath. Her eyes widened. "Look there, Miss Kath—look there—on your dress—"

"Yes, I know. You and Mama pulled so hard on his mouth you tore it. That's Little Plum's blood—his mouth got against my chest. Mama, let's let him rest while I wipe him down.

He's soaking wet. We've got to get him thoroughly dry and it'll maybe soothe him to be stroked."

There was an old cloth in the picnic basket and with it Kath set to work. And the whole time Tiss did not move, having gone back to her fixed stare and occasional whisperings. "But, Tiss," said Elizabeth Rule, "what is it—what *is* it?" Tiss did not answer, and presently she moved over and Elizabeth Rule got up and took the reins from her, while Chattie spilled herself into the back of the cart and huddled there letting out intermittent, lessening sobs.

The last they saw of Tiss, she was walking along her own path as though in some strange place she did not recognize, and she opened her door as wearily and painfully as if she had been beaten.

7  Little Clayton

Kath lay in a state of floating, drowsy comfort. Mama was up and dressing and she could sprawl in the middle of their bed, turning now and then to stretch her legs as far and wide as she liked into some cool, fresh place; never did bed feel so delicious as when she had it to herself and she could lie catty-cornered. But Elizabeth Rule had an eye on Kath, which she was somehow aware of, as though a little point of energetic attention were concentrating itself and could not be disregarded.

"You're going to have to do it sometime, Kath," Mama said finally, pulling up her skirt and buttoning the placket, "so you might as well do it first thing and get it over with. This morning, right after breakfast."

Kath closed her eyes against the pattern of leaf shadows moving on the blinds—shadows trembling ever so slightly in a mere breath of early morning freshness before the already risen sun, spilling its coppery light across South Angela, gathered heat for the day. The sparrows were insanely busy as usual, cheeping and quarreling and flicking themselves about from branch to branch, making a great stir among the leaves.

Sinking into darkness she saw herself get up from the

breakfast table, go through the lobby stale with last night's cigar smoke, greet Ted Morris behind the registration desk, turn to the right out on Main, and go the few steps along to the Sills'. She saw herself hesitate at the door, felt her heart quicken painfully, was aware of sick apprehension at having to face Cordelia. In she went, slipping her hand along the glass counter, then felt it stick and refuse to slide because her palm was clammy. She looked up and there was Clayton, regarding her kindly from behind the cases of combs and toothbrushes, the ranks of lotions and tonics. And she smiled at him and told him in a straight-out sensible way how very sorry she was that he had misunderstood. The fact was, she hadn't at all been trying to make fun of him, but had only been attempting to show that we all of us have our own peculiar habits of pronunciation. For instance, she herself had for a long time thought that u-n-s-h-e-d was pronounced "unsht," which was the way she always said it to herself when she read. To her it fitted the meaning perfectly, so that she was amazed and disappointed when she found out how you actually said it, and still felt that the quick, holding-back word "unsht" expressed much more clearly tears hovering on the brink of spilling over than "un-shed" did. Didn't he? Also, she had, when little, preferred the name "cycropedia" for the letter "g." Funny, wasn't it? She couldn't explain.

"You haven't answered me, Kath. You heard me. And there's no excuse, because Cordelia won't be back until this afternoon."

Kath opened her eyes and suffered an instant of bewildered displacement. Why, she was still in bed and the whole miserable business had still to be gone through. From past experience she had no illusions about her own imaginings: she would have to force out her breathless apology right in the face of the inimical stares of both Sills. For naturally, Cordelia Sill would be home by now.

She stood in front of the drugstore window, the one on the left which had been cleared and dusted and in which Clayton was at this moment placing a most peculiar-looking object. She could not imagine what it was for. It seemed to be a belt, but it had a long cord attached with a socket at the end. It was wide, fashioned of thick leather, and was studded at intervals on the inside with round flat metal bumps, four of them at the back and a very large bump right in the center front. The belt was obviously for a fat person, but now Clayton put a medium-sized one to the left of it and a small one to the right, so that clearly he wished it to be known that a variety of human shapes could be accommodated.

He then disappeared and returned with three impressive hand-lettered cards which he slipped onto little stands near the belts, one for each. And you learned, as you read them, that these were 80-gauge-current Atlas Electric Belts, possessing truly marvelous powers of bringing renewed manhood, vigor, potency, and well-being as well as other exciting benefits—and all for only twenty dollars. Should you be doctoring to no avail, enduring in silence, suffering in secret, you had only to come in and ask for a demonstration. And it was guaranteed that if you wore your belt for one day, acting according to directions, you would feel the first bloom of recovery stealing over you, after only two days realize you were back on the road to manly power, and at the end of one week be completely aware that the full joy of your body had returned and that you need never lose it again.

Clayton must have spent hours over those signs—you could see the guidelines that he hadn't quite succeeded in erasing, the tiny dots at the side that had determined their spacing and the amount of margin, and the painstaking way he had first sketched in his lettering, especially the flourishing capitals with tails to them and flying top strokes, and words like "manhood," "vigor," and "potency," for which he had chosen a different style and that were larger and blacker than the other words.

While Kath and three or four other passersby read, Clayton was busy scattering pots and bottles of mixtures among the belts, mixtures which he must have felt bore relation to general rejuvenation and male attractiveness: Pomade Philacome, "an exquisite dressing for the hair and mustache"; Olive Wax Pomatum, "for fixing and laying the hair, whiskers and mustaches, highly perfumed"; Blondine, "guaranteed to turn gray hair to a beautiful blond"; Old Reliable Hair and Whisker Dye; Eau de Quinine Hair Tonic and Hair Elixir as well as some small rubber objects whose labels proclaimed they were wrinkle eradicators.

Clayton now wafted into the window long loops of bright pinkish-red crepe-paper ribbon tied here and there into large bows from which streamers hung. One bow he tacked up in the back left-hand corner of the window, the second in the middle, and the third on the right. Then, as a final triumphant touch and with a little flourish as if he were pleasantly conscious of his audience, he placed a slender cut-glass vase full of crepe-paper American Beauty roses decked with dark green leaves exactly three inches to the right of the tallest sign, obviously to draw the eye thence.

He had finished. He had created his window.

He looked up, smiled at the little group outside, twinkled his eyes at them, nodded, drew back, and gently closed the sliding doors. Kath heard chuckles and murmurings from the watchers but she still had her duty to do. Somehow, she felt that Cordelia Sill had not yet returned and this feeling grew as she stepped round into the doorway and peered inside.

"Hello, Mr. Sill. Is—is Mrs. Sill—?"

"Nope," said Clayton, beaming at her. Plainly, he bore her no resentment. "Nope—won't be back for a while yet, likely around noon, and here it's all done before she got home, just as I planned. You know what, Kath? I been thinking about this window ever since she left, and I got it all worked out the first night she was away. Laid awake for an hour or more getting it all set in my mind, and the very next morning started to work on my signs. What d'you think? Pretty handsome, aren't they? Y'see, they're laid out strictly according to advertising practice. You emphasize the key words. Did y'notice that? Like *weakness* and *suffering* and *debilitating diseases,* and then *guarantee* and *only twenty dollars,* and *joy* and *bloom of manhood.* Y'know, Kath, I never thought about it before I saw that book on advertising, but it just stands to reason—"

Little Clayton was suddenly no longer aware of her. He was gazing beyond, and when Kath turned to discover the object of his gaze she beheld Cordelia Sill standing in the doorway, her scuffed black overnight satchel gripped in one hand and an expression of blazing indignation written across her face. In the moment Kath twisted round Cordelia flipped the door shut behind her. For perhaps a second there was no sound in the shop but the small whispering hum of the ceiling fan, but that second, Kath remembered later, seemed to stretch out so long that she wondered if it would ever end.

"Clayton Sill," Cordelia said at last in low, measured tones, "you get those belts out of that window this instant. What do you think you've been up to! Do you know what I heard as I came in? *Laughter. Mockery. Derision.* They're laughing at you out there, do you hear me? Do you understand? Laughing at *us.* Somebody sang out, right in front of everybody, 'You and the hubby tried those belts yet, Cordelia?' *You get them out.*"

But Clayton never moved, seeming to be stunned with astonishment. And she could not wait for him, and threw down her satchel and was starting to open the back of the window when it must have occurred to her to wait a bit— to wait until that little crowd had dispersed before she made even richer fools of the Sills than they already were. She stood listening, and it was as if they were frozen there, the three of them, as if, Kath remembered afterwards, they'd been playing a game of statues, until in a moment or two Cordelia peered out, discovered the onlookers had drifted away, and slammed open the back of the window, snatched up one sign after another, and proceeded to tear them from top to bottom.

"Delia—*Delie!*" The tone was agonized, incredulous.

But in a second, so it seemed, the signs were ripped to pieces and Cordelia glared up. Yet as Kath stood pressed against the counter, she felt that she must simply be some anonymous object, for Cordelia's whole being, the entire essence of her, was concentrated unrelentingly upon Clayton.

"You fool," she cried, her voice shaking, "you idiot. I can't leave you alone for one hour. I should have known it. I swear you will ruin us with your childish jokes in front of Mrs. Boughtridge—always trying to be funny, trying to be clever, and you never even notice her expression. And the way you muddle the cash and constantly shortchange us, and now these disgusting signs about potency and manhood. *You* to talk about potency and manhood! We'll be a laughingstock— we already are, you can bet on it. You haven't the sense you were born with and I've always known it, yet I had to go away and leave you, hoping to God you could manage the place for two days—*just two days—*"

There was another silence while Cordelia and Clayton stood facing each other, locked in their searing bitterness. And then Clayton spoke. "You've tore my signs," he said in a voice Kath had never heard from him before. "You've tore them, after all my work—my beautiful signs." He let out a strange little gasp. "I will never forgive you for that. Never—never—"

Kath slipped out of the door and ran away up the street, the sound of Clayton's voice still in her ears and in her mind the look on Clayton's face as he had stood there watching his work being torn to shreds, a face grown small, contracted somehow, his mouth trembling and his eyes drawn up as if he were receiving some mortal blow. It was true what he'd said. Kath knew it. He never would forgive Cordelia as long as he lived.

8 🌿 Tiss Laughing

In the night she heard music rising and falling, flowing and winding, and she thought she was dreaming, that the music had lifted her, whirled her round and round, and she was dancing with Herb, effortlessly, as if she had been born for it, the two of them moving as if they had moved together all their lives. "Sleary music," said Chattie. "Sleazy and bleary—" No, it was not. It was beautiful. "Beautiful!" said Chattie. "It's only the merry-go-round." And Kath woke and she *had* been dreaming, and so it was: only the merry-go-round, set up over in the carnival grounds on the other side of the tracks, but the music of it—from that distance, stealing through the darkness of South Angela where most of the lights were out—haunting, somehow poignant, somehow sad. Yet why? Did Aunt Hattie hear it, and little Clayton Sill, lying in bed beside Cordelia, turning over and over in his mind the scenes of the day? And did it remind them of when they'd been young with everything still to come?

A crash of glass! It smashed across the music and Kath put her hand out and felt the bed empty beside her, the pillow untouched—it couldn't be late. Mama was still downstairs. Then it came again, the sound of glass smashing, and voices raised. Swan was shouting something and, cutting across his voice, the voice of Cade, the new young waiter. There were others, but Cade was the center of a knot of fury. He was shouting accusations, and then Swan could be heard, and lower, yet audible through all the rest—that particular vibrant tone—the voice of Grant. And he went on speaking, and Cade answered with a single word, and a door slammed. Silence. There was the sound of feet running outside, and someone shouted under the back windows, and there were voices over on the far side, under the trees in the alley next to the Sills.

That would be Mama and Grant. Someone had been cut and Grant was going to get Dr. Franklin, and he would come and sew up the wound and put a bandage on. It had happened before, in summer when the heat closed in and tempers rose, and Mama could not have managed without Grant. "I would leave if it weren't for him—I would have to." Was it Swan again, and would he be fired, or Cade? Who had run off? Who had been cut this time? Kath got up and leaned out the back window, but all was silent. There would be no use dressing and going downstairs, for neither Mama nor Grant would ever let her in the back when there had been a fight, when perhaps rage still seethed and Swan would be cursing—or perhaps Cade, cursing and bleeding with his cheek laid open.

"No," said Elizabeth Rule when she came up at last. "It was Swan, and he cut himself—not Cade. A fight between them, and Swan began throwing things and cut his own leg. Cade's gone. I doubt he'll be back." She stood at the window in the dark, looking out, listening. "Why, it's the carnival," she said, "the merry-go-round. Already, when it seems only a little bit ago since last time—" And then, "Thank God it isn't Swan who's gone. I don't think I could—" No need to finish, for she and Kath remembered the same thing, that other morning after Swan left—Sunday morning, and he had set the pies out the night before on the big central kitchen table before he'd taken it into his head to go, and when Elizabeth Rule came down she had found them heaving with cockroaches and she had had to throw them all out and call Tissie at six-thirty in the morning and the two of them made fifteen more before noon, besides getting all the other food ready with the help of the two kitchen girls. Mama said the hotel would have to be fumigated—everybody told to leave—but old Boughtridge said he wouldn't have it, that she could put insect repellent around, and Mama told him that in that case he could find himself another housekeeper. It was fortunate, she said afterwards, that he had taken her at her word.

They'd never come alone before—Herb and Kath. She had always come with Mama or the Jamesons, but all Elizabeth Rule had said was, "Don't keep her out past ten, Herb. Now, remember—I trust you."

How *not* trust Herb? It would be like not trusting Grant. In the firefly darkness he had her by the hand and as they jostled their way toward the first tent, she heard, from the midst of the crowd up ahead, Tissie's high delighted laughter. It couldn't be anyone else. No one laughed like Tiss, who loved carnivals, fairs, circuses, festivals of any kind. Now she would be happy again, here with friends no doubt, for Grant wouldn't be off until late.

"Shall we go on the merry-go-round first, Herb?"

"No, let's wait—it's over on the other side—"

"What's sleary music?"

"I don't know. What *is* sleary music?"

"Sleazy and bleary. Let's play a game. You next."

"Well, what's a—what's—oh, I can't think of anything,

Kath. I'm no good at that." He was too happy to think. He wanted just now only to *be*. "Come on, let's try in here." And he put his arm around her and drew her over, and in the dark, she thought, you wouldn't guess his hair was white—it could be blond—and you wouldn't notice his eyes. He was happy as Tiss was happy, sending up her plume of laughter. He had Kath at his side. He would be paying for her; she was in his charge. Now he held out his money and they pressed their way into the tent to see The Baby Who Knows Everything and The Oldest Human in the World, who was a fortune-teller.

But the Baby was nothing but a dwarf dressed up in baby clothes, perched in a highchair on a tacky stage, and when he answered questions, his eyes, sitting like raisins in their dark sockets, narrowed, so that his worldly little face appeared more worldly than ever, more terribly knowing and hard under the frilled baby cap, and while he listened to the question, he would bounce his little hands up and down and begin to quake with silent amusement, and then his feet under the long baby clothes edged with soiled lace would bounce too, and he would stare straight at the questioner, point a tiny finger at him, and come out with an answer at which the audience, for some reason, roared with laughter. He was a real card, this Baby. But Kath couldn't get the answers, or enough of them to make sense, the dwarf spoke so quickly, shot back his replies in a kind of jeer as if he were somehow getting the better of his questioner, holding him up to ridicule, and with a satisfied smirk on his painted lips shaped into an incongruous bow, pointed to someone else. "Why did my wife —" something or other, spoke up a young fellow at the back; it was a fumbling, halting question, and "Ask the hired man!" rapped out the dwarf. His eyes closed, his painted mouth gaped in silent laughter and he frantically beat his little hands together as though in ecstatic self-applause. Everybody thought this excruciating, Tissie too, apparently, laughing clear and high, and Kath craned to find her but it was hopeless in the shoving crowd.

Now, incredibly, Herb's hand went up and the dwarf pointed. "How many will there be in my family?"

"None," said the dwarf instantly, "because of the old one," and never stopping to give his silent laugh or beat his hands together, went on to the next.

"Herb," whispered Kath, "Herb, let's go. I don't like it—" and they pushed their way out of the crowd over to where the Oldest Human sat in a dark corner in a shelter draped with dirty rugs, and while they waited for the person ahead to come out, Kath looked for Tiss, listened to hear her laughing, but she must have gone. "Why did you ask him? He's hateful—"

"I don't know. My hand went up and the words came out before I could stop them, even though I knew the answer."

"But what did he mean—the old one?"

"The first albino in our family—"

"But how could he have seen you from where he was?"

"I don't know. Perhaps he didn't have to."

"He never hesitated. He didn't even seem to really look at you."

"But he was right. I will never have a family—"

"You said you wanted to keep your books for your children—"

"It was a stupid thing to say. I knew I would never have any children—I would never hand on my hair and eyes to any child. And you can't adopt them unless there's a mother and father. A single person can't."

"But maybe you won't be single, Herb—"

"Oh, Kath!" he said. *"Kath—"*

"But you're too young to be sure of anything like that— to be thinking about all that."

"Am I? No, not too young. You are. But then you're not like me—everything will be natural for you. Because I'm unnatural I think about these things. You can take so much for granted that I can't."

Now it was their turn to go in and sit across from the tiny figure behind a table with a lamp on it—no cards, no magic globe, nothing. The head of the old woman was shrouded in a scarf and when she looked up it fell open, and Kath saw that she must be older even than Chattie's great-aunt, who was ninety-one. But in her eyes was a quiet melancholy instead of that mindless, beady restlessness Kath had always been aware of in the eyes of Aunt Phros. She held out her hands, the backs strangely darkish as if they had been burned by the sun again and again until the skin had been hardened to leather. She apparently wanted to hold Kath's hands between her own and when Kath sat down and offered hers, she felt them taken between two hard little claws, very light and trembling and fragile.

"What is it, girl?" came the faint voice. "What is it you've come to find out?"

"About my journey—the one to the Green Mountains. Will we ever go, my mother and I?"

A smile lighted the old woman's face for an instant, then faded. They sat there in silence and presently Kath began to be overwhelmed by a sense of chaos and confusion, an enormous inconsolability which she could not have explained. And it seemed to last—how long she had no idea—until, muddled and unhappy, she realized that her eyes had been closed, because now, after an undefined length of time, she raised her head and opened them and found the old woman studying her.

"Yes," and the old one nodded, "you will go on your journey. But remember, child, even if you get what you want, nothing is ever as you imagine it will be."

"And Grandmother will be there?"

"Oh, yes—"

"And will we come back?"

The old woman sat huddled in her swathings, looking down as though asleep, still holding Kath's hands in her own. And after a little, "I don't see you coming back. I see a train, and many people, but no station. The train stops, yet there is no station. But you will go on your journey." Another pause, longer this time, then sternly, "That is all I can say."

Kath, leaning forward, caught a whiff of the old, old breath. "But why has the train—I don't understand, when there's a station in South Angela—"

"Please," the old woman said with intensity, "you must go. That is all for now," and Kath drew back her hands, and when one of the fragile claws remained open Herb put some money into it and they went outside.

"Why didn't you stay?" Kath asked him.

"Because I've had my fortune. I don't want any more."

"There is a station at Grandmother's, Herb. I know—I remember." She remembered everything, despite what Mama said. And it was in her mind to try to explain how deeply satisfying it was to her that these mountains she had dreamed of, lofty and green, swept with cool winds—that heavenly vision—should actually have been named the Green Mountains. The beautiful rightness of it! It made what she remembered real: the magnificent valley, its high seclusion, the large airy house which she always saw as being quite isolated and where her room awaited her on the second floor (had done since she was four) with its white bed and the filmy curtains blowing out on a view the length of the valley. All that against Mama's saying, "But it's a small valley, Kath, rather rural, and the mountains aren't lofty at all, more like hills, really, and there are other houses—it's a little community. Grandmother's place is ordinary. I can't imagine how you've got the idea of two stories. Oh, there's an attic—but why don't you write her and settle it? You've only to ask." Yes, of course, she had only to ask. In her next letter she would—perhaps. But why did she dream always of that same house, that same valley? Surely there could be in your memory only what has actually been seen, and she had seen it all so plainly, time and again. These dreams, taking place inexplicably at different seasons, had a reality no others ever had; she could recall them afterwards in the most vivid detail when the usual flow of dreams slid away and were forgotten.

Now she and Herb were standing at the gate of the Race Through the Clouds and Kath could make out, up ahead, that Tiss had got into the first seat with someone—into the car that swooped ahead of all the rest into nothingness—but who she was with Kath couldn't tell; her brother Jink, most likely.

"Come on, Kath—"

"I don't know—I've never been."

"Oh, come on. It's fun, though this isn't anything to the one in Columbus."

But it was terrible, so terrible that Kath, crushed against Herb's shoulder, did not know how she could take, no matter how tightly he held her, one more wrenching jerk after the slow, clacketing climb before they were again thrown headlong into another fall, sent plummeting, when her stomach was left behind and they were flung into space, and the whole time she could hear Tissie's clear, excited cries, triumphant, with not a scrap of fear in them, as if she called on these black depths to take her, and she had wings and was flying into them of her own eager will and could not have enough.

Kath wanted to be sick afterwards. Herb helped her out

and took her over to the side of the carnival grounds, but she only sat there nauseated, and presently began to laugh. "Did you hear Tissie, Herb? Maybe I could get used to it, dropping into space. I'll bet Tiss can take anything—"

He pulled her up and held her by the shoulders. "And here I was going to buy you pie and ice cream and lemonade, and we were going on the merry-go-round—" But its music was no longer alluring, haunting, bewitching, as it had seemed to her in the night. Its sound filled the ears, brassy and insistent, along with the popping and shooting and snapping that issued from the little booths, and the same tune played over and over, da-da-da-*da*, da-da-da-da-*da*, da-da-da-da-*da-a-a-a—da-a-a-a—da-a-a-a*, and there was a pervading smell of burned gunshot powder and food frying.

Inside another tent Madame Olga was dancing the dance of the seven veils. There were creaking old folding chairs tilted in staggered rows along the rough ground and, after Kath and Herb sat down, Kath saw Tissie come in and it was Cade she was with—Cade, shorter by a head than Tiss and beside whom Tiss looked like a queen. Sly, sleek, busy little Cade! As Madame Olga unwound her veils to the tinny music, vaguely Arabian, Kath saw Tiss's upturned face and how she watched with her tulip lips slightly open. Madame Olga peeled off the last veil and was revealed, rather stout, in a flesh pink union suit and corset, hands delicately extended and one knee crooked modestly over the other. Boos and stamping and hoots—what a cheat, what a sell!—while the music rose to a blast and ended on a crash of cymbals.

"Did you enjoy yourself, Kath?"

"Yes—but I got sick on the Race Through the Clouds—"

"And did you see anyone?"

"Only—" Kath looked away and drew a strand of hair across

her eyes. "There was an old, old woman who told me we're going to Grandmother's, you and I, and not coming back. Mama, there *is* a station, isn't there?"

"You mean at Grandmother's? Of course there is—don't you remember? And after you get off the train you have to walk with your bags up a long hill, and then you walk down a little way and around a curve—and there you are."

When the dance of the veils ended and Tissie and Cade got up, Kath was remembering while Elizabeth Rule turned out the light and drew the curtains back, she had looked across at Tiss and smiled and lifted her hand, but felt her smile hanging on her lips as if it knew it wasn't wanted. She couldn't tell if Tiss saw her because Tiss's expression, though she had been looking in Kath's direction, never changed.

9 🌿 A Kind of Cowardice

Elizabeth Rule had stopped by and was sitting with Dr. Franklin and his little boy for a few minutes before coming over to the family table, but she kept looking up and around to see that the new waiter, Harry, was managing his station smoothly. Cade had never come back, and somehow Kath hadn't been able to bring herself to tell of seeing Tissie and Cade at the carnival.

Dr. Franklin, Kath noticed, starting in on her salad, was leaning forward in order to speak very privately to Mama and she, especially beautiful, Kath thought, in the light of the small table lamp with its pink shade, was looking at him with an expression of amazement, her chin resting on her folded hands, her elbows on the table. ("Don't put your elbows on the table, Kath—how many times must I tell you!" but Mama was not being served. Apparently, for some mysterious social reason, this made all the difference.) After her amazement had died, she would turn every now and then and say something to the little boy, Danny, but he only studied her with his large black eyes, watchful, quick-moving like an animal's in his small pinched face, and said nothing. Dr. Franklin wanted to marry her. How Kath knew this she wasn't sure, but somehow she had picked up the conviction from bits of conversation between her mother and Margaret Jameson—a word here and there, certain looks exchanged between them, and Mama would smile to herself. All of which meant, of course, that Elizabeth Rule must have told him certain things about her life or else he would never have presumed to speak. Every time Kath met him on the street he would stop to inquire after her "dear mother." "Take good care of her, Kath," he would always direct with feeling, and had once gone so far as to observe, "She is a very *rare* person." It was Elizabeth Rule's tiredness that made him so anxious, he said, but there was nothing he could do, nothing he could give her, no pills or potions, that seemed to do her any good because she would not follow his advice to get more sleep and rest. If she would marry him, Kath could imagine him confiding to Mama in the privacy of his office, there would be no need for her to lift a finger for the rest of her life in any way she hadn't a desire to. When Mama said not long ago that she'd been thinking of finding some doctor over in Springfield or North Angela, "Is it because it's embarrassing the way Dr. Franklin looks at you?" Kath had asked. "He does want to marry you, doesn't he?"

"What on earth makes you ask that?"

"Doesn't he?" Elizabeth Rule hadn't answered. She would never lie about anything, Kath noticed, but found it possible to divine the truth when her mother was silent or in one way or another evaded answering. "If it weren't for my father, would you?"

"Kath, this is a pointless conversation."

"But *would* you!"

"No, of course not," said Elizabeth Rule sharply. "What an absurd question. I can't imagine it—" No, thought Kath, you couldn't believe she would: that nice, dull, clean, scrupulous man, maddeningly slow in his movements and manner of speaking. Very deliberate, so that you were always wanting to exclaim in exasperation, "Well, go on—go *on!*" After all, Kath said, you usually knew exactly what he was going to say.

"You're wicked, Kath, when he's so good—"

"Yes, but he makes me want to howl."

He lived, widowed, with Danny and Danny's nurse and the housekeeper, Mrs. Doon, in a tall narrow house painted battleship gray and set behind sycamores, the whole kept up with such extreme neatness as to smack of duty rather than that loving attention to detail that you felt in Mason's work at the Jamesons'. And inside, where Dr. Franklin had his office, all was absolutely speckless, every object precisely in place with nothing ever left lying about, and the rooms rather darkish because of the enveloping sycamores. If you left a magazine down, it was whisked away by Mrs. Doon and returned to its place. The wastebaskets were always empty. Sometimes, when Kath went by on her way to the library or to knit washcloths and socks for the soldiers, or roll bandages at the Ladies Aid, she would catch sight of Danny's pale face at a window on the second floor. If a twist of fate were to give him to her as a brother, she would have to listen for who knew how many years while he struggled to make himself understood by means of a box in his throat through which he gasped and breathed and sent out strange, inhuman sounds that, miraculously, his father and nurse and the housekeeper seemed to understand.

Once Elizabeth Rule said with a glint in her eye, "It wouldn't hurt you, Kath, to have a little brother to watch out for. You've no one to think of but yourself." What could she have meant by that? Could she have been testing? And Kath had tested in her own mind which would be the worse, to stay on here at the hotel or to go and live in that battleship-gray house with Danny and Mrs. Doon and Dr. Franklin. As far as she could see, there wasn't much to choose between the two.

But, "You will go on your journey," the old woman had said. "And will we come back?" "I don't see you coming back—I see a train, and people, but no station—" How could that be? What did it mean? But they *were* going, the two of them, she and Mama. *They were going.*

"And I believe that," said Kath. "I believe it." Which put Dr. Franklin right out of the question.

Now it was late, almost eleven, and Elizabeth Rule was sitting at the little wicker desk writing a letter to Grandmother. "My own darling," she would have begun, because she had never ceased to feel the greatest tenderness for her mother and never failed to write her a page or two once a week. "My own darling: You would have been so amused—there was quite a commotion in the dining room this evening. The most odious little man—" She was in her thin silk kimono, and Kath had wrung out the sheet and strung it up with the fan going behind it, but it was so suffocating that every now and then Elizabeth Rule would lean back in her chair and pass a hand across her eyes and give a sigh of exasperation. Kath, sitting up in bed reading, turned her pillow to find a cool place, but in two minutes it was as hot as it had been before.

"Mama, you do believe what the old woman said, don't you?"

No answer. Then, after a little, absently, "I don't know, dear. What do you mean?"

"What I *told* you—about our going up to Grandmother's—"

"Oh, Kath, don't be silly," murmured Elizabeth Rule, scarcely paying attention, her pen never stopping.

"But it's *not* silly. That old woman knew. She was telling the truth—I could feel it from the way she talked to me—"

Kath looked down, trying to read. Face the truth; that was what Herb said you had to do. Face the truth and it helps somehow—with sad things. Never fool yourself. So then maybe they'd never get out of here, out of this one brown room with its tan walls and battered woodwork, the rug so hard worn that what had once been roses were trodden now to a dust-colored blur and, outlined in cracks in the ceiling right over their bed, the earless hound forever fleeing with its lips drawn back in a terrified grimace and the hunched bird gripping its back. I could paper this room, Kath had thought from time to time, but with the idea of their journey so strong in her mind—the ache for it—she had no enthusiasm, having some notion that it might keep them here: to make the room in any way less ugly than it was. Elizabeth Rule's presence was unmistakable—her pictures on the walls, the few books she owned between bookends on the desk, and always flowers, brought her by Aunt Hattie or Margaret Jameson, on the dresser. But nothing could make the room any larger, or change the furniture or the woodwork, or shut out the smell of cooking around dinner time here at the back of the building, nor the smell of old coffee grounds and wet chicken feathers when Swan left the lids of the garbage cans loose and cats and dogs got in at night. Elizabeth Rule sometimes got up and slammed the rear windows even if it meant they could scarcely breathe. She got after Swan, and Grant would check on the lids before he went home, but those cans tainted the air during the hot summer months.

"Mama, tell me again. What are the names of the trees at Grandmother's?"

"Spruce, balsam, cedar, hemlock, pine—" recited Elizabeth Rule, lifting her head and saying the words as though recalling their fragrance, something treasured in childhood, lost at the time she had left the house in Vermont when she was twenty, and never recovered except for one brief visit when

Kath was four. "The trees of the northern woods."

Kath got off the bed, went to the bureau, and found the little fat pillow stuffed with pine needles that Grandmother had sent her and that had "I pine for you" printed on one side. She took it back and smelled it as she read. It had always surprised her that as the years went by the fragrance of the needles never diminished, but Elizabeth Rule said they were probably the needles of the balsam fir because they were the most fragrant.

Now she was aware that her mother had stopped writing, her pen poised over the unfinished letter.

"What is it, Mama?"

"Clayton—I haven't told you. He's gone. You know what Cordelia's been telling everyone, that he's been in Springfield on a business trip, but it isn't true. Dr. Franklin's been up there and saw Clayton, and Clayton's made up his mind he's never coming back. No wonder Cordelia's been so silent. Where he's going he wouldn't say—just out west somewhere —because he wouldn't want to be followed. Dr. Franklin thought he really didn't know himself."

Kath absorbed this astonishing news, turning it over in her mind, picturing to herself that unbelievable moment—little Clayton Sill lighting out after all these years. "But I knew he'd never forgive her," she said presently, "even though I never imagined he'd have the courage to actually pack up and go away for good—"

"Have the courage, Kath! But it's not courage. It's more another kind of cowardice not being able to stand up to someone like Cordelia, never being able to answer back when she insulted him in front of everybody, never being able to keep his dignity and self-respect. Yet what else could he have done, being himself, but run away? I suppose even that took every ounce of spunk he had."

Kath stared at the opposite wall, her eyes widening. *Not*

courage, but another kind of cowardice. "Well," she said at last, her heart quickening, "well, at least, Mama, he had *some* sort of courage, because he's not putting up with her anymore. He's not like you."

Elizabeth Rule laid down her pen. There was a second of silence, and then, "What on earth do you mean?"

Kath twisted herself a little on the bed, curling her legs under her so that she could face her mother, and she could feel her heart thudding and the blood beating in her throat because she knew that now, right now, she was finally going to say the precise and absolute truth. "I mean going on and on no matter how you hate everything, no matter how hopeless it all is. I've been thinking about you, Mama. For a long time now I've hardly stopped thinking about you—about *us.* You're not afraid of anybody, of saying exactly what you mean. You're not afraid of Uncle Paul. You as good as told him to mind his own business that last time he tried to run you because you're his sister-in-law and he thinks he has the right. You're not afraid of Mr. Boughtridge, even though everybody else is. You're not afraid to tell the salesmen, when they make a racket in their rooms at night playing poker, to quiet down, and if they get loud again, you keep after them. And I think you positively enjoyed putting that awful man in his place down in the dining room when he was so rude to Grant. But you're afraid of my father. Yes, you are! You've got to be or you'd never go on working in this ugly, stifling old hotel, not being able to save money because you have to give most of it to him so we can never have a decent place to live but just have to go on in this hole of a room. You're not afraid of anybody else in the whole world—only him."

Her mother sat looking at her and Kath saw her lips move as if she were about to speak, saw her eyes darkening as if anger were gathering. But she said nothing.

"And something else," Kath went on, never heeding—

unable now to heed, knowing only that she must pour out all the rebellion and resentment that had been burning in her. "We went to the farm that day, and there were two little dirty rooms with the animals on the other side of the wall, and he said he was going to build on and wanted us to come and live there because he said he's lonely. *Build on,* when he can't even do anything with what he has and all the money you give him goes for nothing. I've heard you say it, Mama— I've heard you tell Aunt Lily. And you'd have to try to keep that place clean, and work in the fields, and I'm supposed to walk five miles to school and back when there isn't even a decent school and what would I do in the winter? But he never notices me—I don't exist—only you. He said he has to have you with him, but how would there be any money then? And he threw the mice in the fire—I saw him do it. I'll never forget it. He took the lid off that iron stove and just dumped the mice out of the wire trap right into the flames, and they squeaked. They made terrible little noises, but he didn't care —he doesn't care about things like that—and I don't understand how you could have had me with a man like that. I don't understand how you could have done it, how you could sleep in the same bed with him when you don't love him— I know you don't. I've seen you push him away—"

"Kath—I forbid you!" Elizabeth Rule's eyes were dark with indignation. "That's private. I won't have you speaking to me like this about a matter that doesn't concern you—about my private life—"

Kath could feel her throat tightening, her breath coming short. "Doesn't concern me!" she gasped. "But I'm here, Mama, I'm *here,* because of what you did. How can you ignore me? My father can't stand me and you know it, because I interfere—because I take money he could use, because I'm around when he wants you to himself, because probably if it wasn't for me having to go to school he could maybe *get* you to go out to that farm. I don't know—but I do know that when you leave us alone together in this room he just sits there in that big chair and follows me with his eyes—never says a word but just watches me until I can't take it anymore and have to go out. And I *do* matter. You and my father had me and I'm part of this family—you're the one who made it concern me, because you were willing to give in—and maybe still do—to someone you don't love. *Did* you ever love him, Mama? *Did* you?"

Elizabeth Rule's eyes had been blazing straight into Kath's but now the blaze died and her gaze wavered, dropped, and she rested her elbow on the desk and her closed eyes on her hand. There was silence after Kath's question, and then, "I don't know," she said as if she were thinking back over all that happened. "I don't know—perhaps, just for a little, when we were first married." Another silence, and then in a low voice as if telling herself what had been in her mind for a long time, "He thinks he can force what he wants, force anything, *force, force,* the way he fools himself, the poor, deluded man, that he can force that wretched little farm to yield what it hasn't got when anything it ever had was drained from it years ago." She stopped, seemed to reflect. "There've been times when I've felt so sorry for him. God knows, his failure has never been a lack of effort, but always something twists in his hands."

"And then there's your pride," said Kath.

"My pride!"

"I heard Uncle Paul say once to Aunt Lily that you have too much pride to admit defeat, to admit you've made a wrong choice."

Elizabeth Rule gave a small, ironic exclamation. "And did Aunt Lily agree?"

"I don't remember."

"Well, he was mistaken, as he so often is about human motives."

"Then *what?*" demanded Kath fiercely. "If you don't love my father and you won't go and live on the farm because it would be hopeless, and we never have any money, why don't you do something about it? Then we could save and go to Grandmother's and you could get rested—"

"I can't, Kath—I can't—"

"Why not? *Why* can't you?"

"Because it would kill him. I've tried to tell him, but I keep wondering if in some way I'm to blame, if in some way I've put him at a disadvantage, made him feel impotent, futile—incapable." She looked at Kath. "There's so much you can't know, that a child can't know."

"Then you care more about him than you do me. Yet you love me and you don't love him. I know—I've got eyes to see. You're doing what's easy—you don't want a scene, no matter what happens to us, no matter how long we have to stay here, and we'll never get out—never!"

Elizabeth Rule's lips were set, with the white line round them that always came when she was caught in some overpowering emotion, and she was looking at Kath with an expression Kath could not understand. Then she turned her eyes away and would not answer and so Kath lay down on the bed with her face to the wall and did not try to read any longer because she knew it would be useless.

10 🌿 Jason Rule

"Oh, yes—Tiss and Cade, over at the carnival," said Aunt Maud. "I saw them myself. And after Grant firing that cheap little good-for-nothing. Or at least I suppose it was you did it."

"Cade wasn't fired, Maud. He left. Besides, why shouldn't you see Tiss at the carnival with him? She probably met him there and they walked around together. I can't see anything so extraordinary about that—"

"Oh, you don't, don't you! Considering Cade? But you always did stick up for Tiss." Aunt Maud was silent a minute, watching Kath and Elizabeth Rule putting the linen away. "What I think is, Tissie Grant needs children to keep her out of mischief."

"Who says she's *in* mischief?"

"Think what you like. And if she can't have children, why don't she and Grant adopt one or two? No reason. Those families out there litter like rabbits and I'll bet there's a lot of extras don't have known fathers."

Kath added to a pile of pillow slips while she simmered herself into a reply. "Most of Tissie's friends have four or five children, but I know two white families that have eight a piece and the Jenkinses have ten. So what about *that*?"

Aunt Maud regarded Kath from under a high, narrow brow

and her pale eyes were full of a kind of irritated amusement. "I don't recollect, young one, that anybody asked for your opinion. She's getting to be right smart, isn't she, Elizabeth?" Elizabeth Rule went on working. "Anyway, I wouldn't be taken aback by anything, I can tell you. All you have to do is recall the state of those quarters upstairs in the attic when you first came here. Those *chamber* pots!"

"Oh, what have chamber pots to do with *anything*, Maud," exclaimed Elizabeth Rule. "What have they to do with you seeing Tiss at the carnival walking with someone you don't like? Your mind certainly takes the most peculiar turns. Tissie's as clean as any woman I know, and in any case, she never lived in when she worked here. And tell me something. Have you ever been in the public toilets in a city train station? They're vile and you know it." Elizabeth Rule whipped two more sheets into the cupboard with a sharp slap.

Aunt Maud gave her a funny little look, a kind of suspicioning look, Kath thought, with something scornful and puzzled in it. "I don't know what to make of you, Elizabeth, the way you take offense over the oddest things. A person can't hardly have a sensible conversation with you on the subject of Negroes without you getting your dander up. I'll never forget you wanting to turn the dining room here into a meeting place for the help and their friends of a Sunday afternoon in between lunch and dinner before Mount Tabernacle was built. Funniest thing I ever heard of—no wonder Boughtridge had a fit."

"So he did," said Elizabeth Rule. "But he gave in, and it worked out just fine—no offense to anybody. They made far less noise than the Elks or the Rotary or the Lions, and we didn't have to listen to 'Roar, Lions, roar!' nor suffer the stench of cigar smoke afterwards."

"But of course," said Aunt Maud, just as if Mama hadn't spoken, "I always stick up for you, Elizabeth. I've heard one or two call you a certain name, but I never will stand for that."

"Really? That's very kind of you. But you might tell your friends—if it's 'nigger lover' you refer to—that I find it hard even to like some people, let alone love them, no matter what color they are."

Kath had already gotten into bed, and Elizabeth Rule was in her nightgown and was about to take off her kimono when they heard the unmistakable footsteps coming along the hall. Other men walked up and down, yet the instant Kath heard them—that particular tread, quick, with a certain dig of the heel—she knew, and her heart plunged, and Mama instantly wrapped her kimono around again and flicked over the sash and knotted it. She was standing at the foot of the bed with her hand on the rail, watching the door, when it was unlocked and opened and Jason Rule came in. He glanced at Kath. "Hello, Elizabeth," he said, and let fall his old battered suitcase which would be stuffed with dirty laundry. He stood there for a moment looking at her. "I want to talk to you," he said, and without another word made for the bathroom, peeling off his jacket, tossing it over the chair Mama used at the desk, and beginning to haul down his braces. The door shut behind him.

Elizabeth Rule never moved. Kath sat up in bed. "He's *early*, Mama," she whispered. "He's *early*—" She thought she couldn't bear it.

"I know. And I haven't a room for you. I don't know what to do. *Why* couldn't he have let me know!" She picked up his jacket and slipped it onto a hanger in the wardrobe and put the old suitcase against the wall where it wouldn't be tripped over. Then she sat down in the big chair and they waited, not saying anything, until the sound of flushing could be heard and Jason Rule came out. *And he hadn't even opened the window*. But, no, the window was already open. Kath, hunched on the bed with her arms around her knees, watched him with bitterness.

"Well, Kath," he said abruptly, "come on—get your things and go into the other room." He might have seen her only this morning for all the warmth in his voice, in his squarish, weathered, red-brown face and stone-gray eyes with the flat lappet of hair pressed straight across his forehead. But she did not want his warmth; she wanted nothing of him. She stayed where she was.

"Jason, you didn't let me know you were coming, and there's no place for her to go—"

"Well, what am *I* supposed to do?"

"*What are you supposed to do!* Why couldn't you have written me? I can't just suddenly—"

"Don't tell me this one-horse town can fill up a hotel—"

"This town has nothing to do with it, and you know it. It's summer, and the hotel is full."

Jason Rule paced up and down, his hands plunged into the pockets of his shabby old trousers, and he seemed seething with frustration, with resentment, with a burning impatience. "Let her go to some friend's, then—"

"At this time of night? Just ring somebody's bell? *Because you couldn't bother to let me know?*" Suddenly Elizabeth Rule was enormously angry, and as it always did under the power of her anger, her voice deepened, took on penetration and force. "You are incredible, really incredible. You come at any hour you please with never a word, simply unlock the door and come in without knocking, and expect arrangements to be made instantly. Well, you're going to have to find a room somewhere—"

"Then let her go into the bathroom and stay there until I've finished talking."

Kath went cold with outrage and disgust. "I will *not* go into that bathroom."

Jason turned on her. "You will do as you're told—" but already Elizabeth Rule had gone over to the bathroom and was drawing back the curtains. "Come, Kath. Come along. You can bring your book."

"I will not. I will *not*."

Her mother leaned against the doorway and put her hand to her forehead. "Jason, it's so pointless, sending her in there. Nothing is gained. You know that. I'll get dressed and we'll go for a walk, and we can find a room for you—"

"No, by God. I'm not going out. I'm dog tired."

Elizabeth Rule gave him a strange, searching look. "Then there is nothing else for us to do," she said quietly. And Kath saw something in her face, that pale ivory face with its dark eyes and level brows, which in this instant overwhelmed her so that she got off the bed, picked up her book, and went over to the bathroom, closed the door, put down the toilet lid, and sat on it. I should have gotten pillows and a blanket, she thought loathingly, so that I could arrange myself in the bathtub.

She heard the bed creak. "Come here, Liz. Don't sit over there looking at me like that. I've thought of nothing but being here and talking to you. Come beside me—"

"No, Jason. I've been thinking too, and it's about Kath. You hardly look at her when you come in. You've never loved her—never had the slightest feeling for her. No wonder you don't care whether she can hear us or not, *what* she can hear. She's never existed for you, and doesn't now. Not as a person. You simply want her body out of the way so that you won't have to look at her, so that we can be physically alone in this room if not actually. The actuality of Kath doesn't matter to you—doesn't concern you. And I've known that—" Elizabeth

Rule's voice stopped for a moment. "I've *known* that—and yet I've—"

"I didn't come here to talk about her."

A silence. "I'm sure you didn't—"

"We were happy before she was born—"

"We were never happy."

"That's a lie!"

"Jason, why have you come? What is it you want?" He answered in a low voice; he seemed to be explaining something and the explanation went on and on. It had something to do with opportunity, with money. "But you can't mean it," exclaimed Elizabeth Rule. "I think you must be mad. More land, when the land you have is useless to you. What have you done with it? Nothing. What could you do with more land that couldn't have been done with what you have?"

"—*faith*," Kath heard the bitter, grating voice explode. "You've never had any faith in me. Not as long as I've known you—that's been the whole trouble. My God, all I'm asking is two or three hundred. That's all, and it's a bargain. I'll never get anything like it again—"

"I have exactly twenty-five dollars." The bureau drawer opened, which meant Elizabeth Rule was getting her purse. "There you are—" and she was either giving it to him or putting it down somewhere.

Another silence, and then, "What good do you think that'll do? I never expected you to hand me the money. You can borrow it from Jameson. After all, aren't they your bosom friends? Don't you have tea there, go to dinner, go to parties while I'm sweating my guts out on that God-forsaken—"

"I never asked you to. Nobody has ever asked you to do any of the hopeless things you've chosen to do: anything but getting a job that would bring in some sort of dependable income. That's been your decision, the way you've wanted to live—never cooped up, never stuck to the same chair year in and year out. Only, as it turns out, somebody's always having to keep you going—" Again the bed creaked, and then Jason Rule's feet sounded on the floor. "No, Jason, leave me alone. I have something to tell you, something I should have told you long ago. Listen to me—I've got to say it. I don't love you, Jason, and I want a divorce."

Kath shuddered, the convulsive shudders beginning in her belly, gripping it as though it were being taken in a fist and squeezed, and then shaking her from head to foot. She grasped herself in her arms, one arm over the other, and leaned over her book until her forehead touched her knees. She waited in this position.

But there was nothing to be heard in the other room, until finally—an awful sort of scuffling.

"Jason—Jason—"

"I won't let you," he cried in an almost unrecognizable voice. "I tell you I won't let you, Liz—"

Kath leaped up and snatched open the door and her father was trying to take Mama in his arms and she was struggling, pushing him away. "Listen to me, Jason. Please listen—"

"I will not give you a divorce—"

"Then don't. It won't matter. Because I'm leaving you anyway. I don't care what you say. I don't care what you do. I'm not going to see you again—"

And then Jason Rule did a most terrible thing. He suddenly ceased to struggle with Mama. He stood there, his hands at his sides, and Kath saw his chest heaving up and down, and knew that he was crying. And then all at once he crumpled to his knees and put his arms around Mama's legs and leaned against her. "Please, Liz—oh, please. I love you. That's one thing—no matter what I've done or said—I've always loved you."

Mama reached down and pushed at his arms, tried to get hold of them to push them away, to get herself free, but he clung to her and presently she gave up and simply stood there.

"Get up, Jason," she said. "Get up. It's no use. I meant what I said. You might as well get up now, because I am not going to change my mind. You can't make me change my mind no matter how you cry and plead, or try to force me. You will never force me to do anything again, and nothing will ever be any different between us than it is now."

Finally Jason Rule stumbled to his feet and sat in the big chair with his head in his hands and Elizabeth Rule sat on the bed, looking at him, waiting for what he would do next. After a while he got up, like an old man, and his face, Kath saw, was all blurred and shiny. Elizabeth Rule got up and took his coat out of the wardrobe and he turned, as if he scarcely knew what he was doing, and let her help him into it. He stood a moment longer while he got out his handkerchief and wiped his face, then walked slowly over to the desk and stayed there, looking down as though at the money Mama had put on it. Then he reached for it, shoved it into his pocket, picked up his old suitcase, and opened the door. But before he went out he twisted round.

"I will never allow you to divorce me."

"That is up to you, Jason," she said. "But you have no wife. Remember that."

He stared at her for a moment, then he was gone, leaving the door open behind him, and Kath heard her father's footsteps receding down the hall, only now, had she not known, she would never have been able to guess they were his.

Elizabeth Rule cried quietly, making scarcely a sound. She and Kath were in bed and the light was out.

"Why do you cry, Mama? *We're free.* Now we can do whatever we want—"

"I think it must be relief. But something else as well—
it was cruel—"

"*He's* been cruel. And never thought a thing of it—"

"But what chance will there be now for him ever to change?
He will never change."

"You couldn't do it—"

"No, I never could."

"Was it my fault? Did I make you decide?"

"I'm not sure. For a long time I've realized I was going to
have to come to it."

Did you? asked Kath silently. Then what made you keep on?

11 🌿 Why?

Aunt Lily pulled the pins out of her cartwheel straw with the flowers and the black velvet ribbon around the crown and tossed it onto the bed. Then she curled up, pushing the pillows into a comfortable position and held out a hand to Kath. Kath, leaning against her, caught a whiff of fragrance. "What is it?"

"Lily of the valley, of course. Paul got it for me at Sill's. Oh, what an expression—don't tell me you think he's incapable of it." She had to laugh, and Kath was struck all over again with the impossibility of ever penetrating the mystery of a man like Uncle Paul. Reported oddities, such as this one: buying perfume for Aunt Lily, were beyond her. Aunt Lily looked down and smoothed her flowered dress. "Do you like it, Liz? I made it." She looked over at Mama, sitting in the big chair, and there was something sparkling and secret in her eyes. "Now I have to begin making all sorts of things."

Elizabeth Rule regarded her sister with a kind of waiting expectancy. "Yes, Lily?"

"First I want two boys and then a girl. Or will it be the other way round? Only think, Liz—after all this time! Are you happy for me? Say you are—"

"Oh, Lily—how could I not be! I've always wanted for you whatever would make you happy."

"And Pillow?" asked Kath somberly. "Uncle Paul wouldn't—"

Aunt Lily put her head back against the bedrail and closed her eyes. "I am not going to worry about Pillow. I refuse to worry about that—it will be all right. I prayed that I should have a child, and my prayers have been answered, and just so I will pray that God will take care of Pillow. Pillow is a perfectly healthy, beautiful cat who is very dear to me, and I can't believe that Paul would deliberately—that he would actually—no, I think he'll be made to see—"

Kath and Mama waited, and then, "You have great faith, haven't you, Lily?" said Elizabeth Rule.

"But Paul and I have been married for over seven years, and whoever would have imagined that now, after all this time, we should have a child! I've always worked by faith, haven't you?"

"I would hardly say so," answered Elizabeth Rule dryly. "Or at least if I've had any, it's been in the energy of my own efforts. I can't pray any longer, Lily, expecting that there is some kind, elderly presence somewhere who is constantly concerned that my wishes should be paid attention to—considered on their merits—and who bestows rewards for good behavior as if he were dealing out prizes—"

"But He knows when the sparrow *falls*, Liz—"

"Oh, Lily, Lily!"

"If each man in the war," said Kath (she and Herb had had it all out), "if each man who's been wounded or killed prayed to be saved—not to be blinded, not to be blown up, not to have his legs shot off—what good did it do?"

Aunt Lily had drawn herself away so that she could turn and look Kath full in the face. She was silent for a moment.

"But there's a *reason,* dear. I mean, for all those poor men in the war. Don't you *see? There has got to be a reason.* Something beyond our reckoning. And if there isn't, then there's no sense—no sense—and I couldn't bear it."

"I suppose," said Elizabeth Rule, "there seems little sense to me in putting the cart before the horse—putting what I've got to believe, in order to bear, in front of what I see as the truth of the matter: that no miracles are going to be worked. I can't fool myself with some structure of belief I've accepted or made up because I have got to have it whether or not there's a grain of truth in it. Should I have prayed to God to make Jason a different man? And would He have answered my prayers if I'd prayed earnestly and believingly enough? In any case, I've just asked Jason for a divorce."

Aunt Lily, for a moment, seemed unable to take this in. "But, Liz—why did you have to do *that?* I thought—"

"Thought what?"

"That—that you could just simply—"

"Cease to see him? Keep up some sort of dignified front?" Elizabeth Rule got up and started pacing. "Lily, in the name of heaven, what do you understand? This is not a separation, not anything delicate or tasteful—how could it possibly be, considering the nature of Jason! There is only one thing he would understand, and appearances are not to be kept up. I want to be divorced—cut off. I want never to see Jason Rule again. I want him no longer to come to this hotel, or run the risk of his expecting to sleep here, in this room, in this bed—" The words came rushing out as if they had been pressed back for a long time, and as Elizabeth Rule walked toward the bed, with her hands gripped together in front of her, she was looking not at Aunt Lily and Kath, but at the floor as though she were telling herself these things—not them.

"*Liz,* not in front of Kathryn!"

Elizabeth Rule stopped in her tracks almost as if startled.

Then she turned and went over to the big chair and sat there for a moment staring away, and when she spoke again she did not look back at Aunt Lily. "Kath understands more about my marriage than you do, which is only natural. More than I thought she did. What she didn't understand, it turns out, was her own mother. I've been a fool, Lily, if I haven't been wicked. Why not admit it?"

"But I don't understand," cried Aunt Lily, sitting up suddenly, "how you could allow Kath to be a part of all this sordid—"

"Sordid? Yes, I suppose so. But it would have been more sordid to have gone on as before. Kath was right—*that* was the unworthy act, the demeaning—going on when I knew better. And she was already a part, as she had to point out to me. Perhaps she knows too much, but it can't be helped, under the circumstances. I had to earn a living some way, somewhere, and possibly didn't choose wisely, ending up in one room, which at the time didn't seem a drawback, when Kath was six. Yet she seems to have great good sense. No, I can't see how living here has harmed her—really harmed her, in the way Cordelia Sill keeps insisting—"

"I've only hated it, that's all," put in Kath, not wanting to miss the chance.

Aunt Lily got off the bed, picked up her hat, and went over to the dresser, where she put it on and stuck in the pins. She considered herself. "I think a person should be happy while she's carrying her child," she said. "Yes, I know how it was for you, Liz, but it can't have been good for you. And if I possibly can, I'm going to be happy the whole time for the baby's sake. And now let's go down to lunch and talk about something pleasant."

Mama took the material Margaret Jameson had given her out of the bureau drawer and held it against herself, studying the effect. "I don't understand why Tiss didn't come this morning to wash my hair. I can't remember when she's missed. Have you seen her, Kath? I was going to ask her if she'd make this up for me."

Yes, Kath said. Saturday she'd seen her.

"And did she say anything?"

"Not much—nothing special."

Tiss had been across the street, walking along in that swinging, long-legged way of hers, as if she felt better than anybody else in the world could possibly feel, holding her head up and looking over the heads of other people at something off in the distance. "Tiss—Tiss, where've you been? I haven't *seen* you—"

Tiss had stopped and glanced over at Kath, then looked away. She shrugged. "No place special. Oh, been busy at church, making curtains for the social hall. Things like that."

"Did you ever get your rug, Tiss? The one for the center aisle?"

"Sure did, and it's a beauty. Garnet color—pretty as a peach." She lifted her arm, easy-go-lucky, as though to say "So long," but didn't say it, and turned and walked off. And for some reason she could never have explained to anyone, Kath felt there was a great distance between them, far wider than the street.

"Winsome," Mama had called Tissie once. "What's winsome?" asked Kath. "Gay and appealing—" Yes, that was Tiss. Open and full of fun, though sometimes another mood could steal over her when she was remote and brooding, shut up inside herself, and somehow you couldn't just lightly ask, "What's the matter, Tiss?" because you knew she wouldn't tell. She had her own thoughts and they were hers alone and would remain so; she was very private. Yes, but in all these years of knowing Tiss, Kath had never once felt coldness from her, or indifference. Remote she might be because of her broodings, but Kath had never been made to feel that that remoteness had anything to do with her, never felt anything inimical from Tiss. Yet this, though Kath couldn't bear to frame the thought, was what she *had* felt, unspoken, in Tiss's continued progression along the street with scarcely a pause, her few unsmiling words, her vague wave of the arm. But she didn't in the least feel like talking about it.

She woke in the breathless night and was aware of a far-off muffled confusion she could not place nor make any sense of. Somebody yelled in the street; there was an urgent, answering cry, then a repetition of it, tailing off behind the hotel as though the answerer were running in the direction of Willowtown. She noticed a dancing movement on the sheet hanging at the foot of the bed, a vague, rosy ghost of something which she stared at, trying to understand. Now she caught the smell of burning and with extreme care slipped into the narrow corridor between the bed and the wall, ran silently round to the big window near Mama's side of the bed, and saw a pyramid of flame flowering in the night sky.

She stood staring and figuring. Yes, about five or six blocks away, out beyond the end of town and, that big, it couldn't be anything but Mount Tabernacle. Sparks flew up out of the flames, and now the shape of the spire was revealed, crumpling, tottering sideways, where it seemed to hang suspended before it plunged and was lost.

Name o' God! That's what Tissie would be saying. *Name o' God!* Their beautiful white church, four months old, with green shutters and slender white steeple, and the one tall stained-glass window on the east end behind the pulpit where you could feast your eyes on it, especially when the morning sun poured through, lighting up the Lord and the bright emerald grass scattered with flowers, and the blue sky behind flocked with white clouds, just as if the scene itself had its own private sun, and you'd sit there thinking how all the people in that church had put their money together year after year until they could afford what was needed, the timber lengths and the glass and the paint; and then the men, the ones who had callings for all the different kinds of work, turning their hands to whatever they could do best, and up went the church. And while it was being raised, from early morning to early morning, from evening to evening, whenever the men could come, was the happiest time of their lives, Tiss said, except maybe that first day of gathering under their own roof. There they were in their new clothes sitting along the glossy pews in their own church. Their houses could be small and shabby and derelict, in need of paint, but Mount Tabernacle was beautiful, and it was all theirs, everything they'd seen in their mind's eye since the first dollars were gathered.

Tiss had invited Elizabeth Rule and Kath to come. And here was Grant, ushering in the broad center aisle in hickory-striped trousers and frock-tailed coat with brocade down the front, and the tucked shirt Tiss had made for him, and a black bow tie. Ever after that he wore this suit of clothes to direct the people to their tables in the dining room at the hotel, but only on Sunday, because that was a special day and he could come over to the hotel right after Mount Tabernacle. Never had he looked so handsome as on that first morning in the new church in his new outfit, ushering the people to their places. And when he stood up with Tiss and the others in the choir and, after some joyful piece, they sang "When They Crucified My Lord," it took Kath by storm. She hadn't expected this, how his voice would gather up all the rest on a river of power that could do whatever it chose with flowing ease, soar up under the roof from some place out of the depths that Kath hadn't known existed in him, a place of burning sorrow.

Quietly she got into her clothes, opened her notebook and wrote, "Gone to the fire think it's Tiss's church. Back soon don't worry I'll be with Uncle Tede or Herb," and put it in the middle of the floor where it could not be missed. Willing that no board should creak, she reached the door, turned the key, and drew back the latch. At that moment Elizabeth Rule flung an arm across where Kath should have been, but did not lift her head from the fan of hair spilled over the pillow. Now she drew her arm back, turned over, and did not move again. The latch spoke as it returned. Kath, in the gloom of the hall where one dim light was always left burning for latecomers, stopped breathing to listen. Nothing was to be heard inside their room nor anywhere in the hotel except for a steady, muffled symphony of snoring from behind the doors along the hall.

Downstairs, Doug, the night clerk, sat behind the desk on his high stool reading a newspaper in the midnight deadness of the lobby. And when he bent his head Kath slipped into the side entrance and stood for a moment watching from behind the arch. If he heard her it was entirely possible he would send her back. But no, he got up and went into the office, and Kath opened the door and slipped outside and ran.

She looked up through the sycamores as she passed along the side of the hotel, but it was still jetty black up there in the end room under the shadow of the trees. An almost full moon, hanging in the sky over the fire, was bronze colored behind the smoke, and the smell of burning was acrid and heavy. Others were on their way. The dark streets were full of the whisper of scarcely seen movement, women walking hurriedly and speaking in low, excited tones, and the men and children running. Now and then one would yell to another, or someone would call to her, but she kept ahead on her own because she wanted to go with Herb. But his house was silent and unlighted and she was afraid to call up to him.

When she got past, over on the Willowtown side, she saw that his window stood wide open so that he might already have climbed out, dropped onto the scullery roof, and be at the fire by now.

She ran the rest of the way, and came to the church when it was still fiercely blazing. She pushed through the crowd to the front and stared around in astonishment. Where was the fire brigade? Though there was constant movement in the crowd, no one in the inner circle seemed to be doing anything but standing in a trance of quietness, the dark or rosy faces uplifted in awe or in anguish, according to the color of skin, though now and then some black woman would be overcome with a frenzy of grief and send up loud, compulsive wails, a kind of soul chant that came out in wave upon wave of stricken sound.

Presently Kath saw Tiss and Grant not far away, Grant with his arm around Tiss and her own arms crossed beneath her breasts while she stared expressionless at the flames. Kath went to them and saw the tears slowly welling from Tiss's eyes and rolling down her face. She slipped her arm through Tiss's but Tiss never moved nor responded in any way. "Grant, what happened—how did it start?"

Grant shook his head. "Arson, mostly likely."

Where was the fire engine? Broken down over in North Angela, he said, a block or two after it had started out.

"Name o' God," said Tiss presently, so low that Kath only just caught the words. "Why? *Why?*"

For Tiss and the rest of Willowtown, Sunday *was* church. For her and Grant it meant morning service, then when Grant when off to the hotel, Tissie taught Sunday school. Then maybe there'd be a picnic in the woods, then the young people's meeting, then night service, "all of us Willowtowners," Tiss had said once, "kept busy as yard dogs the whole day through."

Tiss was famous for Sunday school. Everybody said so. It was as if, the minute she started telling a Bible story, she *saw* the whole thing right there in front of her. The power in Tiss's voice, the urgency of her raised hands and the way she used them with their long, agile fingers, the light in her enormous eyes shining straight out first at this child, then at that, froze her audience. Kath had seen the goose bumps rise on the children's arms as she spoke and sometimes it would be too much for one of the little ones and he would burst into tears and she would snatch him to her, hug him close with one arm, and surge right on with her story.

Tiss, now, after her question, "Why? *Why?*" said no more, and after a while, when the flames were abating and the east wall, with the stained-glass window, had fallen to a heap of smoking rubble, a hand was slipped into Kath's and she turned and stared into Herb's face. And the sight of his inhuman eyes, illumined red by the fire, so shocked her that she could only say his name and turn her head away. Out of a strange defensiveness she did not want anyone to notice him as she had just now seen him, looking like some kind of evil magician, and she turned from Tiss and pulled him into the crowd. She must go back, she said. Mama might have wakened and be worried.

The streets were quiet and the moon, having sailed clear of the smoke, poured down its hallucinatory light. They walked into islands of shadow and out again into a sea of silver, and presently Kath put back her head and looked up. "Who could have done it, Herb? Who *would* have done it? Burned that beautiful little church? *Why* would they?"

"No reason, maybe," he said, very low. "That's the terrible part. Somebody mindless, doing it for no reason at all, except for a passing pleasure. Maybe it was kids roaming around, getting into mischief. Maybe it was the wiring. Likely we'll never learn." And then, so suddenly it startled her, he reached out and took her arms, slid his hands down them until he held hers and brought them together in front of him. He stood looking at her, and then all at once, "I love you, Kath," he burst out. "I have to tell you some time. I love you." She couldn't speak, for there would have been no words she could have found that would be right, nothing that could answer, that would not fail utterly, the intensity of his emotion. "You don't want me to tell you, do you? You don't want *me*—"

"Please, Herb—"

"But why? Why can't I say it? Because you can't bear to look at me?"

"It's not that—it's not. I never think about it—"

"Yes, you do. Back there at the fire, when you first turned—"

"But it was only the flames reflected in your eyes just at that instant. It made them look so strange, as if the fire were inside you. But usually I never think about it, the way you're different. Honestly I don't. You're just yourself. But it's not that. It's that Mama and I are going away. You remember the old woman said we would, and now I know it's going to happen."

He stood there looking at her in silence. "When?" he asked finally.

"I don't know. Mama's going to get a divorce if she can, but no matter what, we don't have to stay. Now everything will be different."

He still held her hands, his gaze resting on her face with an expression Kath could not read. "I see," he said, his voice barely audible. He dropped her hands and started walking again.

"Herb, don't *say* it like that."

"I can't help it. You're the only friend I have, the only person I really care about outside of Uncle Bob in England. And if you're not here, then nothing's any use."

"But there's *got* to be some use—"

"Yes, well—there isn't, and that's the way it is. I've just got to stick everything until I can get out of here. Three more years—"

"But where *to*, Herb—where *to*?"

They had come to the hotel and sat down on the side steps, quiet for a moment, and the moonlight drifting through the sycamores lay in luminous irregular patterns on the sidewalk and on their faces and hands.

"To England," he said in a low voice. "Uncle Bob said once he hoped that some day I could come over and visit. I didn't think much about it at the time, but now I've got to plan. I've got to. One of these days I want to start all over, fresh, where nobody'll have known me ever since I was a little scared kid and ashamed of myself for being scared. Maybe you think I've forgotten what happened that day when we were in the first grade and you stood up for me—tore into that bunch of yelling demons and began hitting out right and left. I'll never forget that as long as I live—I thought you were a wonder, a little fiery wonder, and you always have been. But I don't feel about you the way I do because of that, and I never hated you for what you did, though it's one way it could have turned out. It's just because you're yourself. Because you're Kath." Now he was quiet again, and Kath waited for him to go on, feeling no need to say anything in return. "I asked Uncle Bob once if he kept writing me out of pity, and he answered that he wrote to me as a friend because my letters interest me and keep him wanting to write, not because I'm his nephew and an albino. He said I'd just have to believe that, take his word he's telling me the truth. And I do, because his letters are marvelous—they can't be duty letters. He's an old bachelor who can do exactly as he pleases and if he wants someone to come and stay, he can do it. I don't know what he'll say, but I've had the idea of going to Cambridge.

He lives there, in the town, and maybe I could stay with him. I've thought about it, but never like now—now that I know you're not going to be here."

Kath sat there watching his face in the half light. Not going to be here. She saw him in his room where the two of them had talked by the hour, where their friendship had been formed. It was a homely room—a portion of the attic not taken up by trunks and old boxes and lumber—with its unfinished walls and shabby bits of furniture, but Kath had always liked it for its privacy and for its sharp woody smell, especially strong in summer when the rafters baked in the heat. It had the air to her of being a kind of eyrie. Two windows, let in as dormers into the sloping roof, one on either side, Herb would open wide and there was a view clear to Willowtown out of one, and of the trees growing thick along Main out of the other.

He'd made himself a desk out of an old table someone had given him, straightened its rickety legs and refinished it, and had made shelves for his collections and shelves for his books where he'd arranged them in some odd, idiosyncratic order of his own. His moths and butterflies were pinned in patterns on cotton wool and framed and hung above his bed. Kath had never known his cot with its faded patchwork quilt to be left unmade, and it was perhaps his pride in his room, his love for it, that compelled his neatness.

When his mother had taken his "little kid books" and given them to the Ladies Aid, and thrown his rocks and fossils over the back fence, what had enraged Kath as much as anything was when Mrs. Mayhew spoke of his "fossil and rock dirt sifted all over the floor" and of his "rubbish squirreled away in the closet." He did not have rubbish—he had possessions. And he'd gotten his rocks and fossils out of the trash behind the fence in the back and recovered his books that the women had been about to give Miss Spooner at the town library. He'd packed them up and brought them home and put everything back again precisely as before, his rocks and fossils on their shelves under the south dormer and, on the shelves under the north, the books his uncle had given him, the ones that had such a fascinating smell Kath could not resist opening them just to put her nose against their pages. "The English smell," Herb called it, that meant something quite personal to him, aside from the contents of the books. Kath had always felt it was because of his uncle's thought for a boy he'd never seen.

Presently she leaned forward. "But, Herb, where will you get the money to go?"

"Save it. I've got to save for college anyway. I'm going to get all the spare jobs I can. I'll be really thinking about it now. Everything will be for that, for going away. Everything's going to be different." He turned and looked at her. "That's what you said, isn't it? That everything was going to be different. So you've made it different for me too—by telling me you're leaving." She put her hand out and touched his, and he caught it with his other and held it where it was. "Don't go in yet, Kath. Stay a little longer."

"For a few minutes, then, but I must go. She'll wake up— Mama will—and wonder where I am."

But later, when she stood at the foot of the bed, she saw that her mother had scarcely moved. As she went to the window, wondering if the glow from the diminished flames would still be visible, Elizabeth Rule woke. "Kath?"

"Yes, Mama. I've been out—it's Mount Tabernacle. Somebody set it on fire and it's burned to the ground."

Elizabeth Rule sat up and looked at Kath as if she couldn't believe what she was hearing. "But why? What do you mean —'set it on fire'? On purpose? Who would do it? *Why* would they?"

"No one knows. Herb said it could even have been kids,

hunting around for mischief, doing it for no reason. Mindless—that was what he said. Or it might have been the wiring, something gone wrong."

Elizabeth Rule got up and came to the window and stood there staring out toward where Mount Tabernacle had once been. "Tiss!" she said all at once. "Tiss!" Then, "So everything's to be done again." She was still there when Kath got into her nightgown and came and stood beside her. The glow was gone from the sky, from behind the trees, but the smell of burning still hung strong in the night air. There was a sense of movement down there along the streets and the murmur of voices as people all over town came wandering home from the fire. The moon was beginning its descent.

12 ❧ The Windfall Burning

Sometimes, over the way Kath made "a positive pigsty" of their room, Elizabeth Rule could get heated up. And it was because of the ugliness of the place, and the general tension and pressure of trying to keep some sort of order and decency in their lives that the sight of an unmade bed at ten in the morning and Kath's clothes all over the place was enough to send her off.

This morning she swung open the door abruptly, apparently already upset, and when she saw the state of the room, stood there silent for a second while she took it all in, her lips set in a way Kath knew and her eyes sparking. "What in the name of heaven have you been doing?"

"Why, Mama, just getting everything ready for school—"

"*Ready!* It looks to me as if you've been taking everything apart. Why have you ripped the skirts off those dresses?"

"Because they're not right—nothing's right. I have absolutely nothing to wear to school, and I've got two weeks—"

"Get this stuff picked up and put away and make the bed." Elizabeth Rule's voice shook. "I can't stand the sight of a mess at this time of the morning. If I can't have order, I'm lost—and you know that. You know it! As if I haven't enough—" and she walked to the big chair, tossed what was on it over to

113

the bed and sat down, resting her forehead on the palm of her hand and grasping her temples as if she had a splitting headache.

"Mama, what is it?"

Elizabeth Rule did not answer, but continued sitting in the same position. Kath, subdued, cleared her clothes away and then, unaccountably, while she was making the bed, it came over her how she would not much longer be making it in this room—would not finish the school term in South Angela. She turned, overcome with a kind of ecstasy. "Mama, I can't wait—"

Elizabeth Rule lifted her head. "You know we can't go until I've saved. I will not go until I have. Grandmother doesn't have a penny over and above what it takes to keep her." She sat there brooding intensely, though about what Kath couldn't imagine when at this hour of the morning she was supposed to be downstairs absorbed in the running of the hotel. Presently Elizabeth Rule got up and took her material from the drawer and smoothed her hand over it. "And here I am, wanting to spend money—"

"But it's your birthday dress—"

"I know, and I thought—just this one. Kath, would you take it out to Tiss and ask her if she'll make it up for me?"

Something needling and swift, a lightning prick of apprehension, shot through Kath, and she was all at once snatched from happiness to the depths of depression. "But she won't do it—she won't. Why not ask Aunt Hattie to make it?"

"Oh, Aunt Hattie, Kath! Aunt Maud would be on it in a minute and she'd ruin it—you know she would. You could run on out with it before lunch. Here, I'll put the pattern in and the money inside the envelope so you won't lose it. And don't forget to tell Tiss about Boughtridge. He's away now, but when he comes back I'll ask him about the dining room, if the Willowtowners should want to use it again."

Kath, the birthday material in a package under her arm, went miserably up Main toward Toland. She did not see how she could possibly go along Tiss's walk, knock on the door, and ask her if she would make this dress. Not after the troubling mystification of that moment when she'd seen Tiss across the street and asked her about the church carpet and Tiss had scarcely bothered to answer, let alone crossed the street or held out an arm for Kath to run over so they could have a chat the way they'd always done, wandering along saying whatever came into their heads or laughing over some neighborhood tale Tiss had been working up. She always had a new one, something comical that had caught her delighted imagination. She had a gift for seeing these small happenings in a certain way, a gift for telling them, just as she had a gift for telling Bible stories.

No, there was something terribly wrong.

Without being aware of it, Kath had passed the Boughtridges', a heavy mass of red brick surrounded by undeviating borders of hard-colored zinnias and marigolds and with a gazing globe and two black iron deer on the lawn, and had come to the big cream Jameson house sitting on its sweep of green shaded by an enormous elm and several smaller maples that sent their winged seed pods spinning down over the grass and which Mason, the gardener, raked up in their hundreds. From the entrance of the broad graveled carriage drive, Kath could hear Dillis working the vacuum cleaner back and forth in Great-Aunt Euphrosyne's bedroom. Little Plum would never again trot along that drive, for shortly after the train incident Mr. Jameson had taken him back to the stables, where Kath visited him and took him treats.

"Kath?" Here came Chattie, running—actually running—along the drive toward her, and when she got up close Kath could see that her usually melancholy eyes were alive with excitement and that there were beads of sweat on her upper lip and her forehead. "Kath, did your mother tell you what happened at Sill's? She's getting a divorce, isn't she?"

Kath gazed at her in shocked astonishment. And before she could stop herself, and furious the instant she let it out, "How did you know?"

"Because your mother was in Sill's just now when I was in there. Only I don't think she ever noticed me. And when Cordelia Sill saw your mother didn't have her wedding ring on, she wanted to know why, and did it mean your mother's marriage had come to an end? That was the way she put it, and she wouldn't have cared *who* was in there. And your mother said something—I couldn't hear what—and then Cordelia said, 'Well, now, I *hope*, Elizabeth—' you know that tone of hers, 'I *hope*, Elizabeth, it didn't have anything to do with Grant—and by that I mean as a result of your *friend*ship with Grant.' Well, there was the most awful silence, and your mother said, so low I could only just hear her, 'You know as well as I do, Cordelia, that that remark is unworthy of you.' '*Well*,' Cordelia said, and she pulled her head over to one side and hitched up her shoulder the way she always does when she's about to say something mean, 'I don't know what my unworthiness has to do with anything that goes on over at the hotel, when I only know what I see with my two eyes and hear with my two ears.' Right off, your mother turned away from the counter and stood still for a second. Then she turned, and I could just make out that she was reaching over and *patting* Cordelia's hand. 'Cordelia,' she said, 'I know how wretched it must be for you since Clayton went off and refused to come back. We all feel for you—believe me, we do.' And she *swept* out of the store, and I looked at Cordelia and her eyes were sort of fixed and she was trying to say something all the time your mother was sailing out. 'Well, at least—' she called after her, 'well, at *least*—' but she couldn't seem to get any further and all at once I knew it was because she was afraid she'd cry, and I waited for what she'd do next, but she only put her hand up to her mouth and went in behind that bead curtain and I couldn't hear a thing after that so I left. You mean your mother never said a word?"

Kath waited a second or two in order to steady herself. "She's always busy all morning—we don't usually talk until lunch."

Chattie gave Kath a studying look. "Where are you going?" she asked after a bit.

"Out to Tiss's to see if she can make up this material your mother gave Mama."

"All that way in this heat? You wouldn't catch me! I'm going up to the screen porch and have some lemonade, and this afternoon we're going shopping for my school things. We might go into Columbus and stay all night. But Friday Mama wants you and your mother to come to dinner. I heard her telling Dillis."

A suffocating weariness, an enormous resentment in the face of her long and pointless errand swept over Kath and she half turned away. "But I don't think we can come," she said coldly. "We're leaving here and we've got an awful lot to do."

Chattie drew in a stunned breath and stared at Kath. "*Leaving!* You mean South *Angela*? You mean for *good*?"

Chattie's expression was unutterably satisfying. "Yes, for good. Forever and ever and ever."

"But *when*, Kath—where are you going?"

"Up to Vermont, to the Green Mountains, to live with Grandmother, at least until we can find a place of our own. I've told you before that we would—someday, and now we're going. I'm not just sure when, but soon."

Chattie couldn't seem to believe it. "Are you glad?" she asked finally in an odd tone.

"Am I *glad!* You mean to get out of this ugly little one-horse town—?"

117

"It is not an ugly little one-horse town," cried Chattie. "It's beautiful."

Kath looked at her incredulously. Never would she have imagined Chattie to have a thought in her head about South Angela, to have been in the least aware of it as any particular sort of place or to have cherished any special feeling about it except as her comfort or discomfort might dictate. And Kath knew perfectly well that South Angela wasn't ugly, that it was, in fact, at least in part, rather attractive, but she wasn't to be deflected for a moment now that she had the upper hand. "Am I *glad*," she surged on, "to be going up in the mountains where it's cool and green and there are millions of pines and firs and cedars and a view out of my big second-story bedroom window down a whole huge valley! You bet I am!" And without another glance at Chattie she turned and walked away, swung around the corner onto Toland, seeing in her mind with the utmost clarity how Chattie had, earlier, raced along the drive heavy with news as a home-going bee laden with honey and bursting to tell it—to Dillis, to her mother—it didn't matter who just as long as she could get it out: how Kath's mother was getting a divorce and Cordelia Sill said it was because of Grant; and now the second feast of news: how Kath and her mother were leaving right off for the mountains and never coming back—never—but why, do you suppose, *why* were they leaving? Did it have anything to do with Grant? Or with Tiss *because* of Grant? "Hush your mouth, child!" Dillis would be exclaiming, shocked to the core, and she could say this because she'd been with the Jamesons since before Chattie had been born, but this never made any difference to Chattie. Nothing Dillis ever said or did made any difference to her unless it was something to do with Dillis's kitchen, and there the line was drawn. And Chattie would go on simmering and stewing and seething with her news, turning it over and over in her mind and reflecting on it, just as Cordelia Sill did.

Yes, thought Kath, it could be Chattie would turn out exactly like Cordelia when she grew up, coming cool and fragrant down the stairs to her drawing room instead of worn and sallow from behind a bead curtain into a drugstore.

An escaped hen addled its way along the road in front of her when she got out near Tiss's, then ran squawking and flapping off to the side through a fence when Grant and Tiss's black-and-white dog Lucky came bounding to meet her. "Well, somebody still loves me, doesn't he, Lucky?" and she squatted down to stroke him and got her face licked and felt somehow comforted as though Lucky represented Tiss. When she stood up she noticed a spire of blue smoke rising out of Tiss's back garden; she must be burning trash—too early to burn leaves.

Kath went along toward the house through a garden crowded without plan, yet all the more eye-filling for it—roses and syringa and lilac (the lilac blossoms gone by now) and geraniums and hollyhocks and stocks and delphiniums all rioted in together because Tiss liked plenty of color and smells. In spring she always had daffodils and crocuses and narcissus and grape hyacinths coming up near the house, and they would all be mixed in so that the perfume, when you knelt and buried your face in the blossoms, was enough to send you reeling.

When Kath got out in back where Tiss raised vegetables, she saw that Tiss had quite a blaze going, but it wasn't just trash. It looked as if she'd been in the woods and got a lot of windfall as well. But why? On this hot summer day! And now Tiss came out of the house, rather awkwardly because she had a load of something in her arms, something dark, and she had to twist herself and work her leg around to keep the screen door from slamming behind her. She seemed especially not to want that screen to slam. She came down the steps from the porch and along the path, not noticing Kath, who was standing a little to one side in a clump of hollyhocks, and when Tiss drew near, Kath was stunned to see that what Tiss was carrying were three of Grant's law books. And when she got to the bonfire she let two of them fall as carelessly as though they were nothing but old no-account blocks of wood, and began tearing the pages out of the other and throwing them on the fire.

"Tiss!" screamed Kath and dropped her package and made for Tiss, but before she could get to her, Tiss had thrown the book into the flames and snatched up the other two and was about to throw them in as well when Kath reached her, and they grappled together. But in a moment Tiss had managed to fling them in. "No, Tiss—no—!" and Kath grabbed a long stick from a pile of them Tiss used for supports and was stabbing away at the heavy volumes when the screen door was heard and Tiss straightened and in that second or two Kath shoved the books out of the fire.

Kath knew it was Grant had slammed the screen and now she turned and saw him, and she would never forget the expression on his face as he charged toward them. "What're you doin', Tiss—what in the name o' God're you doin'—!" Kath looked at Tiss, and Tiss's eyes were blazing. She stared at Grant, then turned and faced Kath.

"I be sick!" she cried. "I be sick in my soul for Grant'n me, him workin' away all night an' dead durin' the day, an' it's all for no use. That's the flat of it. An' we used to be so happy, him an' me—but not now. We was happy before you an' your mama came bustin' in. What did you want to do it for? What's the use of it? Ain't any use—" and she turned and ran off toward the back of the garden, round behind the outhouse and a row of sunflowers, and Grant squatted down beside his books and picked them up, one after the other, and rubbed them against his trouser leg. The pages were gone forever that Tiss had ripped out and thrown into

the fire, but where the great chunks of books had landed they
had smothered the flames beneath them so that they were
scarcely harmed. Kath went round and knelt beside him.

"They're not ruined, are they, Grant? Only the edges
scorched?"

"Yes," he said, "only the edges." His hands were shaking
as he turned the book he held and opened it to where Tiss
had snatched out the pages. Then all at once it came bursting
out of him as if he couldn't contain it any longer, his hurt,
his bitter indignation, his anger. "*Tiss*—oh, my lord—my lord!"
And Kath knelt there, little sharp stones biting into her knees
but the pain not keen enough to tear her attention away from
Grant's face while she tried to understand what was going on
inside of him. How had he not known what Tiss was up to;
how, in that little house, had she been able to take his books
from him and get outside without him seeing her?

"Grant—!"

He shook his head slowly back and forth and kept shaking
it the way he had at the church fire when she had asked him
how it started. And it came to her then that perhaps that fire
had put this one into Tiss's mind. "I was so dead asleep I never
heard a thing until you yelled 'Tiss!'. And then I smelled
burning and right off something hit me. Don't know what it
was, but I guess I knew right then what Tiss was up to." He
picked up the other two books.

"But, Grant, what are you going to do? Tiss hates those law
books. Now I know what it is about Mama and me. She hates
us for what we've done. And we didn't mean to ruin your
lives. We only thought—at least Mama thought—"

"I know, I know. And you haven't ruined our lives. Your
mama did me a great service and please say nothing to her
about this, about Tiss trying to burn my books. I've got to
explain to Tiss again just how it is with me and that she's
got to be patient. And then I'll talk to your mama myself.

But I must talk to Tiss first. So you won't say anything about the burning, Miss Kath—if you don't mind."

"But, Grant, Mama notices every little thing—"

"Yes, I realize she does. But I'll speak to her—let me do it. And now I've got to go and find Tiss."

Grant went into the house and left his books, and when Kath got out into the road she looked back and saw him headed for the rear of the garden. And it wasn't until she had got a block away that she realized she had left the material thrown down in the hollyhocks, and when she went to retrieve it she heard Tiss shouting in anger over on the other side of the row of sunflowers somewhere not far away in the woods. She couldn't see Tiss and Grant, off there in the trees, and she couldn't make out Tiss's words, but Tiss was beside herself with fury, there was no mistake about that.

"But, Kath, why wouldn't Tiss make my dress? She didn't feel like it—all right. But what's the matter? Something's wrong. *You* feel there's something wrong, and without a word, she doesn't come to wash my hair the way she always has. If she couldn't come before for any reason she would tell Grant. But not a word this time. And when I asked Grant, he said he didn't know. He seemed not to want to talk about it, as if he was embarrassed. What is it, Kath?"

"It's the law books. She wishes we'd never brought them— I think she hates us for bringing them. She says we've ruined their lives because she doesn't have Grant anymore. That day of the picnic out at Aunt Lily's on your birthday, she said they've got him, those books, and when he reads them he goes a long way off. She says he studies all night and is dead during the day. She said, 'What did you an' your mama want to come bustin' in for?' And she said she was sick for Grant and her—that they were happy before but not now."

Elizabeth Rule's eyes were fixed on Kath's face as if she

were trying to pierce through to whatever Kath might not be saying, to what more *could* be said. "Hates us! Tiss hates us? Oh, no, Kath. Surely not—surely she must understand. I can't believe—"

"But she *doesn't* understand—she *doesn't*. She says Grant can't become a lawyer, that it would be impossible. She says there's no use in all this, and that it's a waste. I suppose what Grant's doing is trying to practically memorize those books. She said they used to have such fun—and they did, Mama. It's true."

"But a human being—any responsible human being—can't just have fun all his life," cried Elizabeth Rule. "Will Grant is a man who's been working for years at a job that's miles beneath him with no hope of getting out of it. Has *he* been happy? What in the name of God *is* 'happy'? Don't you believe it about Grant. And Tiss is blind if she thinks her husband's been happy all this time just because *she's* been having fun. It makes me angry just to think about how unfulfilled he is. And what better work for a man like Grant, with the capacity he has, than the law. He's always wanted to be a lawyer. He and his father used to talk about it—it was his idea from the beginning. Tiss should remember that. I can't understand her. I simply can't believe she's had no idea of what's been going on inside of that man, her own husband." Elizabeth Rule got up and began walking up and down as she always did when she was excited or indignant or caught up in some passionate discussion with herself. It was as if any deep involvement would not allow her to sit still—she must exercise herself in every fiber of her being. But all at once she stopped at one of the side windows and stood there looking out into the trees.

"What is it, Mama? Are you thinking about what Cordelia said?"

Elizabeth Rule lifted her head but did not turn, and there

was a little silence as though she were catching her breath. "What do you mean? When?"

"I mean this morning, what she said about Grant. About hoping that—that your marriage hadn't—" but Kath could not go on. The words refused to come.

Now her mother turned and again fixed Kath with that dark, intent gaze of hers. "Who told you what Cordelia said?"

"Chattie. She was in there when Cordelia said that about Grant." Elizabeth Rule's expression did not change. "She said she didn't think you realized she'd come in. But Cordelia must have, only she wouldn't care. She wouldn't care *who* heard."

Elizabeth Rule walked slowly over to the big chair and sat down. "Yes," she said finally, "that's what I was thinking. She's a merciless woman—Cordelia. Utterly merciless."

"But you got back at her. Chattie said she was trying to answer while you were walking out, but she couldn't manage it because she was about to cry."

"*Cordelia?*" Elizabeth Rule stared at her. Then she looked away. "Cheap!" she said. "I was cheap. She brought me down to her level because I so despised what she was saying, her pettiness and cruelty. She knows as well as you do that Grant is the most upright of men, that there isn't a dishonorable bone in his body. And she knows as well as you do that I feel nothing but respect for him, and gratitude. I admire him for the kind of person he is. But as for—oh, my God!"

"But what did you mean—she brought you down to her level? That you were cheap?"

"Taunting her with Clayton's desertion. That's what she could do to me."

"But it shows what kind of woman she is that she *could* do it—"

"Yes, and I let it be done."

"Well, I'm not sorry. I'm glad you said it. I only wish I'd been there instead of Chattie. *I'd* have said something."

There was no answer, and Kath knew what Mama was thinking: that her cool, smiling, falsely kind retort had without doubt only served to deepen Cordelia's spite. "I'm so sick of everything," Elizabeth Rule said all at once. "I'm so sick of it—"

"Then why don't we *go?*" demanded Kath. "It would be so heavenly if we could just go!" Suddenly she was filled with a longing for the green mountains so deep and intense she could hardly contain it.

"Not yet, Kath. I will not leave this town because of Cordelia. I will not. There's no need to keep at me. I'll know when the time has come."

13 🌿 Night Voices

The Buswells' brown, narrow, two-story house was getting shabbier by the year. The porch was beginning to list, it seemed to Kath (or had it always and she'd never noticed?). But considering Uncle Tede's pension and what Aunt Hattie and Aunt Maud got from their dressmaking, nothing would ever be painted or repaired now. The only things attractive about this house were the tough old rose vines that straggled along the fences and burst into riotous bloom every summer, big fat roses that turned pale and let fall their petals soon after they'd opened, the wisteria vine that covered the porch and drooped panicles of deep lavender over the edge of the roof, and the beech whose roots had cracked and pushed up the front walk until it was dangerous, Aunt Maud kept saying, but nobody ever did anything about it and likely never would.

Aunt Hattie opened the front door, and when she saw Kath, her whole face, round and bright pink and damp with perspiration, lighted with pleasure. Her blue eyes brightened as if she'd been given a gift. "Why, Kath! What a grand surprise—come in, dear—come in! Tede and Maud had to go over to Springfield on business and won't be back till nightfall, so I thought I'd get in and finish my piccalilli. Tede and

Maud love it, but Maud can't stand the way it smells up the house when it's simmering, so I usually do it when she's away." She drew Kath in, slipped an arm around her waist, and gave her a delighted squeeze. "Look at that!" she cried. "How you've grown—I have to look up! Why, in these last few months, it seems to me—I can't believe it. I'll bet that's why you've brought your dresses. I know what! I'll make a pot of tea and cut some thin bread and butter and put out the jam—I made apricot last week—and we'll have it all cozy in the kitchen just like we used to when you'd—" She stopped suddenly and Kath knew exactly why, and felt stricken with guilt. She leaned down a little and pressed her cheek against the soft damp one, then turned and lightly kissed it. Aunt Hattie still used Mavis powder.

"I know I don't come by like I used to, Aunt Hattie, but it's just that—"

"Oh, honey, you don't need to explain. Come on, now, out to the kitchen and sit down while I put on the kettle. Throw your things on the chair there and we'll see to them later." She bustled along the dim little hall where the light fell somberly through the green and blue and yellow panes of the front door and a few shapeless garments hung on a coat stand with a couple of Uncle Tede's battered old hats piled on top. "You don't need to explain—I know how it is when you begin to grow up and things change. You get other interests. You're not a little girl anymore, and it isn't very exciting over here—"

"But it isn't *that*—"

"—and Aunt Maud takes on so about everything. I don't know—she's getting very sharp, Kath, very sharp in her old age, and she seems to take it out on me—"

"But she's always been sharp." Kath, out of habit, got down plates and cups and saucers from the china cabinet without thinking about it, and the silver from the silver drawer, and laid two places. "She's always told you to 'See to your potatoes,' or 'Go along, Hat, and see to your roast—it'll need basting about now,' as if it wasn't just as much up to her to see to things as you! It's always made me so mad I could hardly stand it—"

"Oh, I know. It's sort of funny, isn't it! That's always been a joke between Tede and me. But I shouldn't have said anything." Aunt Hattie began buttering the cut top of a loaf of her own baking, then sliced off a piece, holding the loaf against her plump bust as she cut, and continued buttering and slicing until she had a considerable pile. Then she got out the jam.

Here in the kitchen, Kath realized suddenly how long it had been since she'd last come by, ages and ages. And she was aware, as she had always been, of the special smell of this house, one she'd never liked but had always, nevertheless, associated with the peculiar pleasure she'd had as a small girl of coming here and playing in the garden, almost as thickly overgrown in the back, as untended and exciting to her imagination, as the one next door, a garden where she would continue her endless, solitary games from day to day, coming in now and then to help Aunt Hattie with her cake and cookie and biscuit making, taking the little bits of dough Aunt Hattie would cut away from the biscuit rounds, roll them in her grubby hands and put them in the oven for Uncle Tede. And they would come out gray, hard little nubbles which he would solemnly butter and eat because Kath had "made" them.

It was a foody-smelling old house. And the smell, she thought now, was a mixture of something sourish, no doubt from all the chutney, piccalilli, relish, and pickled peaches Aunt Hattie had been concocting all these years and that more often than not didn't agree with her, and the stale cigar smoke that saturated Uncle Tede's clothes. Though he wasn't allowed to smoke in the rest of the house, he would do it up in his room and the smell clung to his suits and crept out under the door.

Aunt Hattie sighed, leaned her elbows on the table, and rubbed her fingers back and forth across her eyes, leaving them red and more wrinkled around the sockets than ever. Then she poured the tea, handed Kath her cup, and Kath spread jam on her bread and butter. They sat in comfortable silence for a moment and Kath remembered how she used to curl up, unnoticed, in the corner of the parlor, drinking her milk and eating one cookie after another while Aunt Maud and Aunt Hattie visited with their ladies come to have their dresses fitted and drink a cup of tea and get on with whatever gossip was going, and Kath would sit there taking it all in, still as the cat, old Thomas, dead long since, lying asleep in the sun.

"I thought when I'd finished the piccalilli," mused Aunt Hattie, "I'd go out and do some gardening. It's a rest to me, to get out there when the afternoon grows cooler, and see to the plants. Working with them, even for a little, does something for me—I don't know what. All the tension goes. But of course I can't do it in the sun." No. Right now, Aunt Hattie's face was flushed. Surely her cheeks were too red, it occurred to Kath, and she was far too stout and had got stouter in the last year. Had she always breathed like this, in short rasps?

"Aunt Hattie, I don't like you breathing like that. Are you all right?"

"Oh, a little high blood pressure and overweight, Dr. Franklin says. I've got to be careful, but I don't just go on working right through if I lose my breath or get tired. I take rests on that old bench over there on the south side of the garden in back. You know the one—" and she flicked a sly, secret, laughing glance at Kath and gave a chuckle, which for some reason Kath immediately understood.

"Aunt Hattie! The one near the fence between here and the empty house?"

"Yes, honey, that one—"

"Then you—"

Aunt Hattie stretched out her fat, short-fingered hand and put it over Kath's, and she was smiling and there was something young and conspiratorial in her eyes. "Don't mind, Kath—don't mind. If you only knew how I've loved it, you having that secret place. I wasn't snooping, but several times when I've been sitting there, enjoying the air and the birds and watching everything, how lovely it is, I've heard that old gate leading into the back alley give a little click, and then there'd be a silence, and then after a bit you'd run up on the porch. The first time I heard it, of course I'd no idea who it was and I was all set to tell Tede to tell the bank people, but then I looked through the hedge and saw it was you. And I was just tickled. I could tell from the way you were standing there up on the veranda looking back into the garden how you felt about it, and then you turned and opened the door, and peered around inside for a moment, and then stepped in. And I said to myself, 'There now, that's her house—at least for a little while.' "

"But, Aunt Hattie, how could you know? I mean, how could you know what I felt! That was exactly it—it always is—"

"Why shouldn't I know? It would have been just what I'd have felt at your age if I'd found such a place, cool and empty and quiet, sitting there by itself ready for me to come and fill it up with whatever I had a mind to—furnish it, live in it, have everything just the way I wanted. No Maud complaining and bossing and watching every last thing I do, and has done ever since we were children, since she first began taking care of me. She sure has taken care!"

"Does she know?"

"Why, Kath, do you think I'd tell? And she's never out there, except for a minute or two to get me back in to start dinner or lunch, or get on with some more sewing. I never tell her a thing, and I wouldn't even tell Tede just in case he might get a notion you shouldn't be going in there."

"Do you think I shouldn't?"

"I don't see it does a bit of harm. After all, what can you possibly do but wander around and pretend, the way you used to out here in the garden when you were little, making up your games and stories. Only I wouldn't go in there at night—"

"At *night!*"

"Oh, don't you, dear? I thought maybe you'd told Herb and you and he had stolen in there once or twice."

"No, not Herb. I've never taken him there. Did you see us the night of the fire, coming home? I looked up and your light was on, and then it went off. I thought you might be standing there at the window after you put the blind up."

Aunt Hattie looked down and tore a slice of bread in two, and then tore the half. "Yes, I did, Kath, and I thought how nice it was that you and Herb should be out together on such a beautiful night. Sometimes I get up and look out on nights like these. But I didn't call to you because if there's one thing I can't stand it's a prying, peering old woman like that Cordelia Sill. She lets nothing pass—there's nothing she doesn't notice or hear about, and I'm getting so I can't stand it anymore. Oh, that woman—but there's one thing I'll say for Maud. She's never told me as much, but I do know that if there's one person she's always admired it's your—" Aunt Hattie stopped and sent Kath the quickest, unhappiest look, a guilty look, then glanced away and bit her lip.

"Aunt Hattie, what has Cordelia told you about Mama? Just exactly what did she say?"

"Oh, Kath—!"

"Yes, I know. Chattie heard her when she and Mama were

having it out. I suppose she's telling everybody Grant is the cause for Mama getting a divorce."

Aunt Hattie gave a cry and put her hands over her face. "Don't say it—don't even *say* it. It's unthinkable. And I told her so. Maud and I were in there together and she started in and we were furious. I don't believe I've ever seen Maud so angry and you should have heard what she said to Cordelia. I positively admired her—she let fly far more than I'd have had it in my head to say, right off without even having to think. We ended up never buying a thing, just walked out. So that's something to cheer you. And keep in mind that the people of this town have a *respect* for your mother, and Maud and I aren't going to let Cordelia's kind of viciousness get any further than here if we can help it. You know, we see most of the ordinary, middle-class people of this place, the women, that is, and they're the ones who carry the word, the poor silly things. About Elva Boughtridge's set, I wouldn't know. Maybe they're worse. Anyhow, you just remember that about Maud and me. And if you want to tell your mama—if you think it would help—you tell her. *I* couldn't bring it up to her. I couldn't begin to." Aunt Hattie drew a deep, shaking breath and looked away, and there was a little silence again while the clock ticked and the house gave a loud creak somewhere. Finally she said, "Tchk!" and shook her head as if appalled at her own thoughts, got up and began putting the plates together, then stopped all at once and leaned on the table and looked at Kath, a little frown coming between her brows. "You say you and Herb, or you and Chattie—oh, but it couldn't have been her, not at that time—have never gone into the garden next door at night? I thought you might have, it's been so beautiful in the evenings, though really, dear, I don't think it's a good idea—"

"But, Aunt Hattie, it's never even occurred to me—"

"Well, isn't that funny. Not long ago I could have sworn I heard somebody laughing, and then voices, rather late. Of course it might have been in the street. Yes, I suppose it could have been in the street. Well, now, let me see your dresses and let's get to work."

14  Chattie

As Kath and Elizabeth Rule came along the front hall after Mrs. Jameson, Dillis stepped out of Great-Aunt Euphrosyne's bedroom with her evening tray, and Margaret Jameson stopped. "Would you both just say hello to her? She doesn't get many visitors and I can't be in there all the time. I think she must get lonely, though I'm not sure she even wants anybody."

Great-Aunt Phros, huddled in a bed jacket against two fat pillows and fluffed about by a down comforter, peered up at them from under bristle brows that had never turned gray and that seemed to grow thicker with age. She grunted as Elizabeth Rule sat down beside the bed and leaned over to greet her and take her fleshless, crumpled little hand.

"How are you, Aunt Phros? Did you enjoy your dinner?"

The old woman pursed her lips and appeared to be thinking over, with the greatest possible seriousness, what answer to give, when suddenly her face darkened and she replied in a harsh voice, "Terrible! Just terrible!"

Mrs. Jameson leaned over the foot of the bed. "Do you mean the way you feel, dear, or your dinner?"

"Dinner! Couldn't hardly get it down—too much salt as usual. Why that Dillis can't remember—enough to make anybody sick to his stomach, but o' course I know why she does it. She doesn't fool me for a minute. 'Tisn't forgetfulness. It's cussedness, that's what 'tis, pure cussedness."

"But Dillis doesn't put a speck of salt in your food anymore. I know she doesn't—we just spoke about it—"

"Rubbish!" cried Aunt Phros in bitter indignation, her mouth trembling. "Rubbish, I say! Couldn't hardly eat a thing. She ought to be fired, that girl. I said it the first week she was here, an' I still say it. Don't know why ye keep her."

Margaret Jameson's face broke into an amused smile. "Oh, Aunt Phros, do you realize how long she's been with us? Seventeen years! Ever since Jack and I were first married."

A look of bewilderment crept over the old woman's face and her mouth fell open revealing a few discolored teeth. Her little pebble eyes darted about as if she were trapped. "Seven—" she murmured, blinking rapidly and seeming to reflect. Then all at once a look of sly mischief replaced the bewilderment. "How d'ye like my room, Elizabeth? Had it all done up—" and she waved a hand about rather jerkily, as if it were on a puppet arm controlled by wires, and slowly raised her head and turned it stiffly from side to side, while Kath tried to remember when this room, with its red plush wallpaper, its heavy draperies and massive Victorian furniture, had ever looked any different. Not a thing, as far as she could remember, had ever been changed. "But, listen—" and Aunt Phros raised herself from her pillows on one elbow and pointed a finger at Elizabeth Rule and Kath, stabbing it up and down a time or two. "Don't you let Jack Jameson tell you *he* paid for it, because he didn't. Never paid for a thing! It all came out o' my purse, just like everything else does around here—always has. Just you remember that." She sank back as if exhausted and nodded to herself, cogitating resentfully. "Every cent," she said, "every single cent. Don't know what 'tis with him—can't seem to make a success of anything. But

I told Margaret, an' she wouldn't listen. Never would—only got herself to blame." Margaret Jameson looked at Kath and her mother and sent them a quick little wink. Then Aunt Phros waved her hand about as if impatient with herself. "But what was it I wanted t'tell ye! Yes," and the pleased, mischievous expression came back and she gave a little breathless cackle. "Ye recall that light spot on the wall there?" She nodded at the wall opposite.

"No, Aunt Phros," said Elizabeth Rule, "I don't believe I do."

Aunt Phros grinned at her and cackled again. "My head hung there—my shrunk head. An' when I took it down because Margaret said she couldn't stand it, it left a light place, so that was why I had the room done up fresh. Anyway, I put the head in my trunk—but 'tisn't there now—" and she went off into a spasm of noiseless laughter, her eyes squeezed shut in exquisite appreciation. "No, sir, 'tisn't there now. I packed it up an' sent it off—" and she laughed until the tears came to her eyes and spilled over onto her lined brown cheeks and seeped into the wrinkles. Finally she gave a gasp. "Oh, dear!" she whispered, and wiped her eyes on the edge of the sheet. "Best joke I ever pulled on that woman in my life, that one was."

Kath leaned forward. "I know, Aunt Phros. I know it was. And they thought so too. Your son and his wife. You remember you sent me, about four years ago, to take the box for a birthday present to her. And when your daughter-in-law opened it she laughed and laughed, just the way you did. She thought it was a fine joke."

Instantly, all the joy vanished from Aunt Phros's face and again her old mouth fell open; her eyes widened in astonishment and she gazed at Kath as if Kath had gone out of her mind. "What's that, girl?"

"I said she thought it was a lovely joke. She hung it up

in your son's study for a surprise. Haven't they told you?"

The old woman's chin crumpled and her mouth drew down like a little girl's who's been slapped. "Won't see 'em," she cried in a shaking voice. "Don't want 'em. Won't ever see 'em!" She stared at Kath. "Y'mean—that woman *liked* it?"

"Well, of course, Aunt Phros. Didn't you mean her to?" Kath could feel the gaiety dancing in her own eyes as she returned Aunt Phros's furious glare.

"Ye're lying. I bet you anything ye're lying, you wicked girl, you. Get right on out o' this room. All o' you. I'm tired to death an' I want to sleep. Now, go 'way!"

"Poor old Aunt Phros," said Jack Jameson, carving the beef at the head of the table. "You'd never believe what a handsome woman she once was, with thick, dark glossy hair and blue-gray eyes and long dark lashes. And I've never seen such a complexion—Celtic, which of course she is." And all at once Kath, sitting there opposite Chattie at the candle-lit table, looked up and *saw* Chattie, how one day she too would be— not beautiful like Mama, but handsome perhaps, with her slightly too heavy chin, her straight nose and large, melancholy eyes with the dark well-shaped brows above. She would look as Aunt Phros had, years ago, and she would be tall and lazy and quietly in charge of her own house. She never answered Dillis's protests or indignations. She would glance at her and turn away and do exactly as she pleased. Kath had an idea she would always do exactly as she pleased.

She and Kath, just before Dillis had come in to announce that dinner was ready, had been amusing themselves as they used to when they were young when Kath had first begun coming: sliding on the thick cream-colored rug with its scattering of leaves and flowers and giving out sparks to everyone they touched. When Kath had been a child she had thought this the most miraculous thing in the world, that a snap of energy could leap from her finger to the other person simply because she had been sliding on a rug. They'd laughed just now, she and Chattie, laughed and been silly just as they used to. And Kath asked Margaret Jameson if it were true that, when she had come here to lunch one day when she was six, she had taken a bite out of a glass, and when they gave her another she had bitten that one too. She couldn't decide if she'd made it up or if someone had told her she'd done it, or if she herself remembered. But Dillis, appearing in the entrance of the living room at that moment, chuckled and said, "Yes, Miss Kath, you sure did—you sure did bite those glasses an' I was scared out o' my wits you'd cut yourself. What a child you was—what a *child!*" and having announced dinner she took herself off down the hall laughing and shaking her head.

And now as Kath looked at Chattie, seeing her as she was going to be, and thinking of how the Jamesons had always included her in Chattie's treats during the eight years she'd known them, she felt a momentary wave of sadness and regret that she would no longer be coming here. Yes, but whether she left or not—it *was* all over. She knew that. She and Chattie might have gone on seeing each other but without any real desire to be together. She did not know why this was so, why it should have happened, but it had.

"What is it, Kath?" Chattie asked in surprise. "Why do you look at me like that?"

Kath was always forgetting how much of her feelings she put into her face. "Your dress," she said. "It's new, isn't it?"

Chattie looked down at herself, obviously pleased. "We got it that day I saw you going out to Tiss's—the day I told you about being in—" and she stopped, but her expression never changed, "—about going into Columbus to get some new clothes," she finished, and calmly took a plate from her father and handed it to her mother, and you would never have guessed that she had nearly opened a chasm.

There was the smallest pause and Kath knew quite well what they were all thinking. Mr. Jameson, who had come in just as Dillis announced dinner, glanced at Elizabeth Rule, then went on buttering a biscuit, and Kath watched the movements of his long-fingered hands, one of them bearing a heavy gold ring. There wasn't a thing about him she would have changed and had often noticed how Chattie seemed most of the time to think very little of him. Chattie didn't know about fathers—she knew nothing! "Elizabeth," he said, "Margaret's told me you and Kath may be leaving us. You can't think how sorry we are."

"I can't believe it!" exclaimed Margaret Jameson. "I can't accept it—I don't want it to be true."

"But it won't be very soon, Margaret," said Elizabeth Rule, and Kath's heart plunged. "I have so many things to decide. If I leave, I'd like to see Grant put in charge. He told me a long time ago that if I ever left he intended asking Boughtridge about it."

Mr. Jameson gave an ironic little laugh. "The old man'd never even consider it, Elizabeth, and you know it."

"But Grant would make a far better manager than I've ever been." She sat there with her chin on her folded hands seeming to think back over her life at the hotel, her failures, her struggles with her own weariness. "All the same," she said slowly after a moment or two, "in a way it would be a disadvantage for him—I mean the eternal responsibility, without letup when he wants to bend every effort toward taking the bar, and the more time he has to study, the better."

"He'll have to go to law school—"

"I know. And how is he to afford it unless he can save—"

"If he got to be manager," said Kath, "Tiss'd be fierce about him giving it up to go to law school. Anyhow, there's no use talking about it. Sometimes I wonder about Herb," she said, to change the subject. "What could *he* do when he grows up?"

"Oh, Herb—!" said Chattie dismissingly, smiling to herself in amusement.

"All right, *Herb*," retorted Kath. "He's got to earn a living some way, and not just any old way—"

Chattie gave a little laugh. "Maybe he could go with the carnival the next time it comes around. I should think they could use him."

Something hit Kath in the pit of the stomach. She met Chattie's eyes and was so stunned she couldn't find a reply.

"Charlotte Jameson," said her mother, "I'm shocked at you."

Chattie shrugged, but her neck was reddening. "Well, it's true. I bet they *could* use him—what's wrong with that? I'll bet he'd have fun."

Her father looked at her. "Chattie," he said in a level voice, "you're cruel. We'll talk about it later, but you are never to utter such a thought again. Never. To *anyone*."

All at once Chattie stood up. She took in their faces in one swift glance and Kath had never seen her so angry. She put her napkin on the table, then looked at her father. "I'm an intelligent human being and I refuse to be treated like a child," and she turned and went out of the dining room and up the stairs.

After she had gone, Margaret Jameson gave a sigh. "I don't understand about Chattie these days, I really don't. One upset after another—"

"The thing is," said Kath, "that if Chattie ever did mention that to anyone, the kids would never forget it."

"That's the whole point," and Mr. Jameson held out his hand for her plate, she gave it to him, and he began filling it with seconds the way he always had.

They stood in the hall at the door. It was only nine but there were still accounts to be gone over at the hotel with Jenny Knowles because it was the end of the month. And as they stood there talking about Kath and Elizabeth Rule leaving, Mr. Jameson said, "You know, Elizabeth, on the subject of Tiss disapproving of Grant wanting to become a lawyer, it might be very difficult for him—"

"Well, of course it'll be difficult. He knows that."

"Yes, but I mean—I imagine they'll work it out somehow —Tiss and Grant—don't you?"

Kath's eyes went from Mr. Jameson to her mother, and she saw her mother give a quick little glance sideways and saw the set of her mouth and knew instantly that she had been going to talk to Tiss, had been going to try to make her see reason.

15 🌿 Don't Do It, Kath

When Kath, outside the hotel, said she thought she'd go on over to Aunt Hattie's to see how her dresses were coming along, she felt that Elizabeth Rule scarcely heard her. The moon had gone just past the full and patterns of silver fell on Mama's face as she stood there, seeming lost in thought. "All right," she said vaguely after a moment or two, "though perhaps Aunt Hattie will be going to bed—"

"Oh, not already, Mama—"

"Well, then—don't be late—" and Elizabeth Rule turned and went slowly into the hotel.

If Aunt Hattie was in bed, it wouldn't matter—it was far too beautiful to go in. She couldn't bear the idea of climbing up to their insufferable room after being at the Jamesons' and walking back in the quiet dark. Yes, but it would be hard to endure the house smell at the Buswells' after the night air. Funny she never used to think about it when she was little, or not enough to bother. And suddenly, because at the same time as the house smell, she remembered becoming aware last time of the smallness of the hall and the kitchen and the parlor as she had never been before, she thought now of something Chattie's father had told them during the evening, and of how it had piqued and troubled her in some way she could not understand.

When he was a little boy he had gone often to Aunt Phros's and had thought her house the most intriguing place he had ever known. His uncle's study was an enormous room with pillars rising here and there, and a vast desk at the end of it in front of a row of windows. From these windows you looked down into a deep, leafy ravine where a brook ran and where ferns and other shade-loving plants grew thick. And there were bookshelves in the study that went up from the small boy's shoulders to the ceiling and there was a stepladder that ran on a track attached to the shelves so that you could climb up; and when you gave a shove you could take a trip along beside the books, which he had delighted to do, pretending to be his professor uncle looking for some needed title, or he would search out something that was full of pictures for himself.

Below the shelves, because his uncle had been an ornithologist, were innumerable drawers filled with stuffed birds, every kind you could think of, lovely things—blue and gray and red and yellow, green, brown, black, vermilion, or colors combined in every modest or marvelous variation imaginable. There must have been two or three hundred drawers filled with the soft still forms, their claws wrung, and each with its fragile, delicately hued or spotted egg beside it. And because of the birds, there was always a fascinating smell in that room —a smell of preservative, but the little boy hadn't known, only that it was an unexplainable part of the enchantment.

In the living room, with its broad stone fireplace where logs vanished during the winter months, there was also a distinctive smell, the smell of the fireplace that hung there the whole year round. At the end of the living room was a sun parlor and in it a big wicker chair with a basket arm in which he would hide whatever book he had got from his uncle's shelves so that he could go on reading or looking at it the next time he came.

His family moved when he was eight, and he hadn't gone back to Aunt Phros's until he was twenty. He couldn't believe what he saw when he once again stepped into that low-ceilinged living room from the front hall. He recognized at once the smell of fireplace—stronger than ever now, it seemed to him—but the room had mysteriously darkened; it was shabby and not nearly so long as he remembered, nor the sun parlor as large and warmly inviting, and both seemed impossibly cluttered. Perhaps the clutter made them seem smaller, but he could not recall them so. In fact he had always had a sense of spaciousness, of ample distance between one piece of furniture and another.

Then, with Aunt Phros trailing behind and telling him all about his uncle's death, he had gone eagerly to the study, filled with an intense desire to re-experience the long-ago enchantment just the sight of that big book-lined, drawer-lined, light-filled room with its scattered pillars that had given it such an airy look, had once bestowed on him. But another shock! For the room that, had anyone asked him, he would have sworn must have been thirty by forty or forty-five feet at least, he saw now as no more than half that. There were not six or seven pillars as he remembered, but two, halfway along. And the vast desk was simply an ordinary one such as anybody might have. He had thought it princely. To ever have a room like that, or such a desk, he had used to tell himself, would be beyond imagining. He could not understand the trick his mind had played. It was devastating.

Actually it had been a quite usual experience, he said. But when he was twenty it had happened to him and seemed then, that incredible shrinkage, some melancholy act of magic.

All was dark downstairs at the Buswells' when she arrived. A light still burned on the upper floor at the back in Uncle Tede's room, and at the front behind the blinds in Aunt Hattie's. She must be reading in bed. Kath looked over at the mass of trees surrounding the white house next door and a peculiar, sudden desire came over her to see that garden by moonlight, to experience it by moonlight—to make it wholly hers. "I wouldn't, dear," Aunt Hattie had said. But why not? She wanted to. Suddenly she was determined, partly because it would be like taking a dare.

She retraced her steps along the block to Main, turned left toward the railroad tracks until she came to the little bushy alley, turned left again and ran along it in the bright white light of the moon. She lifted the latch, held her breath as she opened the gate lest it should creak or squeak, and did not allow it to click when she drew it to behind her. She went peacefully in under the canopy of foliage and, in the checkerboard of light and shadow, made her way to the potting shed and inside, over in the far corner, lifted the pot under which she always hid the key. But it was not there.

She straightened and stood thinking, trying to see herself the last time she had come. Surely she had replaced it. Still, she could not be sure. She went outside and studied the house, a pale shape off there under its cave of boughs. She listened, but no sound came from it. Only now, for the first time, she was suddenly aware of the mad singing of the crickets, thousands of them—*zing, zing, zing, zing!*—in this enclosure of rank growth. She drew a deep breath, made up her mind, and went along the walk and up onto the porch. *Don't go in, Kath. Don't go in. Don't do it.* But I'm not in the least frightened, and I've got to find where I left the key.

She let the screen door close behind her, but left the door itself open because she would only be a minute. A little way along the hall she stood looking, for there was a corridor up between two branches outside the study window across from where the study opened into the hall, and moonlight flooded through to the living room arch. How beautiful it was, and this was what she had wanted to see: how it would appear to her if she lived here and had gotten up in the night, and had come in to—

Her blood stopped. She had heard a laugh; it could only have been a laugh, very low, and if it were Tiss, who was the only one who knew where the key was kept, why should she be laughing to herself in this house, alone? She went forward and looked round the archway and saw an indistinguishable mass of movement on the floor in there in the study—two figures who seemed to be wrestling together in the strangest fashion. And then one of the figures rose up, and in the moon-light, falling in at the height of the figure's shoulders, she saw that it was Cade. And then someone laughed again, and Kath knew it was Tiss.

She stood there in the utmost bewilderment, absorbing what she could scarcely understand, what she refused to understand—yet did, and gave a cry, and turned and fled. And as she reached the door she heard a scuffling somewhere behind her and Cade's angry voice calling out something, she could not understand what, and in a numbness of horror leaped down the steps and ran faster than she had ever run in her life along the dark path. Like a mindless hare she turned in at the black entrance of the potting shed and pressed herself into a corner and crouched there shivering, clenching back the sobs that tried to rise in her throat while she listened and shuddered. No sound. And she knew that she should not have come into the potting shed because she was cornered, but it was too late. She dared not run out now. She had had nightmares like this and knew from experience that she must not.

Presently she heard voices—and it was Tiss and Cade coming along the path and they stood at the gate and argued in suppressed tones. Tiss was telling him what to do and he was protesting, but her voice continued, steady and urgent, and then the gate closed and they must have gone off along the alley. Kath did not move, and she did not intend moving until she figured they should have reached Toland and been well on their way. In fact she would not move for an hour; they must never know—*never know*.

Now the ache in her throat became too much to bear and she began to sob to herself and to utter a name, "Grant! Grant!" The shuddering was becoming more intense and she grasped herself around the middle, her arms pressed against her stomach to ease the pain, and rocked back and forth. And when she looked up after a little, she saw that someone was standing at the entrance of the potting shed, could make out the tall figure against the pattern of light and dark behind it.

"So it *was* you." Tiss's voice was low and cold and hard.

Kath got up and went over and faced her. "Get away!" She scarcely knew what she was saying—it all rushed out. "Get away from me! How could you have done it! I asked you about the old oar joke and you were so pure and high and mighty you wouldn't tell me, and look what you've done to Grant— look what *you've* been—" and Tiss's long arm came out and her palm swung against Kath's cheek with a hard crack, and where her palm had struck, the flesh burned.

"Don't you say nothin' to me about no old oar joke, Miss Button. You did it—you caused it. Don't say nothin' to me. You *or* your mama, an' I can just see you tearin' home to tell her. Can't wait to tell her—"

"I'll *never* tell her—I'll never tell Grant. Not if they were the last people on earth I wouldn't tell them. But I'll never forgive you—ever—ever!"

Tiss stood there for a long moment, and it was only later

that Kath realized she had not seen Tiss's face the whole time. And it was only Kath's voice, her sobbing to herself and speaking the name "Grant" that had given her away. But Tiss must have guessed all along who it was had sneaked into the house, who had uttered that cry at the entrance to the study, sped along the hall and down the stairs, and who would be likely to hide in the potting shed if she thought she wouldn't have time to reach the gate before Cade got outside. Tiss must have known all the time she was standing there arguing with Cade, sending him on his way. She could have made Cade do anything.

Tiss stood without moving, as if studying the black interior of the shed and listening to Kath crying, the short, spasmodic jerks. Then she was gone, and Kath sank down again and did not know how long she stayed crouched there before she got up and went outside, along the path to the gate, looked up and down the alley, then headed for Main. As she ran along the street she remembered Tiss going up the path to her house, having been brought back in the pony cart after her mystifying reaction to Little Plum galloping madly toward the train. She looked as if she'd been beaten, and Kath thought she understood now how Tiss, for whatever unexplained reason, must have felt then.

She put her hand up to her cheek and it was still hot. It must bear the imprint of Tiss's palm and, her face being sodden, she could not imagine what she would tell Mama. She prayed no one would see her. And when she slipped in at the side entrance she knew that Mama and Jenny Knowles were still closeted in the manager's office. The door was open a little and she could hear their voices.

Later, when Elizabeth Rule opened the door of their room, the light was out. Quietly she undressed and went into the bathroom to put glycerine and rosewater on her face and brush her hair, then came out and got into bed. After a while she said softly, "Kath?" But Kath did not answer and her mother put her hand out and rested it lightly on Kath's shoulder. "I know you're awake, dear. What's the matter?"

"Nothing—"

"Oh, Kath, I know you. What is it—tell me. It would help to tell."

"Nothing—leave me alone—" But her voice was hoarse and stifled and wretched and her throat ached intolerably with the effort not to cry.

A long silence, and then, "Is it Herb?"

"*Yes—yes!* Now please leave me alone—"

Her mother's hand tightened for an instant. "I'm sorry, dearest—I'm so very sorry." Then suddenly she slipped her arm around Kath's waist and drew her close, and now Kath was able to cry until she was drained of tears and could find sleep at last, a haunted dream-ridden sleep in which she and Mama climbed the hill with their suitcases and looked down on the big white house, and there were no blinds at the windows and the garden had run riot. And when they had gone along the walk, overgrown with weeds, and up onto the leaf-strewn porch, no one answered the door.

16 🌿 The Train

When Kath came in about five in the afternoon, Elizabeth Rule was lying down with her arm across her eyes. She had a blue letter from Grandmother in her hand.

"How is she? Is she all right?"

"Don't sit there, dear, on the edge of the bed. It makes the mattress tilt. Of course she's all right. Why wouldn't she be?"

"I don't know. I had a dream the other night." Kath looked away, seeing her dream that, like the one in which she climbed the steep side of the mountain and ran across the cool, windswept saddleback and looked down at the big house sitting in its valley, she could not forget in any least detail. "Grandmother's house was empty when we got there, and the garden was all gone to seed. There were no curtains or even any blinds, and the porch was dusty and littered with old papers and dead leaves, and nobody answered the door."

"But she's all right—perfectly healthy and energetic as usual. She's been putting up fruit."

"For us?" It was time she wrote Gran again.

"Yes, for us, though I've told her I've no idea when we can come."

"Have you asked Mr. Boughtridge about Grant?"

"But I'm not ready yet, and I must speak to Grant first."

Kath looked down and was silent for a little. "How is he? I haven't seen him much, not to say anything to."

"Why, how would he be? What do you mean?"

"I mean Tiss—you know what I mean—"

"Why do you harp, Kath? Whatever has happened is between them. What are you worrying about?"

"But I just do worry," said Kath desperately. "I just do, because we've ruined their lives. At least, before, Tiss had her church."

"Ruined!" Elizabeth Rule, who had lifted her arm and had been studying Kath, let it fall at her side. She turned her head away. "Why do you say that? Why do you keep saying 'we'? It is not 'we.' It was I—I who thought Grant should have a chance to do what he'd always wanted. I who bought —was determined to bring the books back with us, not you. But how absurd to say we've ruined their lives. They've had a tiff, a difference of opinion, and it's up to them to settle it." She closed her eyes again and Kath thought, after a moment or two, that she had fallen asleep. But she hadn't. "Grant said Tiss has gone off for a few days to stay with a friend out beyond Willowtown, someone who works for a family out there. They're having relatives to stay and Tiss is going to help. Kath, why don't you go over to Aunt Hattie's and get your other dress. I must sleep before I take my bath. I woke so early—"

Kath got up and went to the door. "Were you thinking, Mama?"

"Yes. Yes, I suppose I was."

"Mama, *did* you buy them?"

Elizabeth Rule did not answer at once. "Buy what?"

"You know," said Kath softly. "The law books for Grant."

"You know I meant 'brought'—"

"But did you buy them?"

A faint color crept into Elizabeth Rule's cheeks. Her eyes,

watching Kath, moved away. "Five dollars—it was all I could give her. Give Maizie. I had to. I couldn't take them for nothing."

"But she said she didn't want anything. She said Tom was through with them."

"But I thought he could use the money, being young and starting out."

"But you told Uncle Paul—"

"Because it was none of his affair! He had no right to ask—it was intolerable—"

Yes, so it had been. And Mama had a right to keep her secret. Kath stilled herself trying to grasp something. Mama had had to do that for Grant, give what hadn't been asked for, money she couldn't really afford, because she—surely not because she loved him in the way Cordelia had accused her, but cared, very deeply, perhaps as if Grant were a brother. No, not that. There was some nuance of feeling Kath couldn't quite lay hold of. "Dearest friend" was the nearest she could come, and perhaps this was it. But of one thing she was certain: Mama had had to give something she herself needed as a sign or token that she believed in Grant. That had been her way of testifying for him.

Kath had started up the front walk when the door opened and Aunt Hattie came out. She seemed disturbed; she laced her fingers together and stood there blinking in the light after the dimness of the house.

"What is it, Aunt Hattie? Is something the matter?"

"I don't know. There's an accident somewhere off that way—" and she waved her hand northward. "But I don't just know what kind. Tede and Maud were out in front here and a man came along and told them about it—I think he said something about the train—and so Tede and Maud just took off with him. That was some while ago, maybe a half hour or so. Why don't you go along and see what it's about. I'd come, but I'm just no good at walking fast—it wouldn't be any use my going."

"But I don't like accidents—" All the same she did not go up the stairs. Something held her.

"All right, dear. Then come on in. I have your dress ready, and we'll have something cool to drink."

Still Kath stood there, her thoughts drawn to the north so that she could not go inside with Aunt Hattie. "Maybe I'd better," she said uncertainly. "Maybe I'll see Aunt Maud and Uncle Tede." She looked up at the soft round face with its troubled eyes. "I'll run and see, Aunt Hattie. I won't be long."

Yet why should she be going? Why? It was true: she could not bear accidents and the people crowding around, shoving each other out of the way in order to get a better view, lusting like hounds over the kill. Sadists and barbarians, Mama called them in bitter disgust. Ghouls. Yet here was she, Kath, ashamed but running, walking quickly then running again, and now she was aware that, like the night of the fire, others must have got some word and were hurrying northeast, one or two here, another there across the street, and some coming from side streets and either going along Maple or hurrying straight on down toward the railroad tracks before they crossed Toland at the eastern edge of Willowtown and wound out into the country.

Finally she ran for almost three blocks and then thought of the little woods, a belt of mixed sycamores and maples, that you could go through just this side of the tracks. All the people were headed in one direction, but there was no use following along the sidewalk, and when she came to the trees she ran into the blessed coolness, knowing she would come out somewhere near where Toland met the tracks.

And no sooner had she entered the grove of trees than she heard something thrashing about just ahead of her, and strange cries, as if an animal were caught in a trap and was struggling fiercely to free itself, or as if some battle were being fought between two animals. The bushes grew so thick she could not see what was going on, but when she had gone a little farther she made out a man lying on his face on the ground to the side of the path and he was flailing about as if in an agony of spirit and was beating his hands up and down and crying out. When she came to him she saw that it was Cade, and she knelt beside him and put her hand on his shoulder. She had gone deathly cold and for some reason her heart began thudding wildly as if, like the animal she had pictured in the trap, it was fighting to free itself.

"Cade—Cade, what is it? What's the matter?" He looked up at her but did not seem to recognize her and reached out an arm and pushed her away. He got up on his knees, bent over, supporting himself on his hands and shaking his head back and forth as if he did not know what to do with himself. And he kept sobbing and speaking words which were unintelligible to Kath, as if he had been speaking a foreign language. "Cade—please tell me—please! Is it the accident? Is it someone you know? Is it one of your family? What's happened?" But again he pushed her away, sobbing incoherently, beyond help, beyond all human communication, and at last she got up and went on her way, and when she came out of the woods she saw the train, with its smoke hovering lazily over the stack, on up the track toward the South Angela station, and there was a crowd of people where the tracks crossed Toland.

As she went toward them, some were turning back, among them Uncle Tede, but he did not see her because he kept looking round as if expecting Aunt Maud to come along. She was there, still at the edge of the crowd talking with a little group, so Uncle Tede walked away toward Kath and then he looked up and saw her and stood still while she went to him and he put his hands on her shoulders.

"Kath," he said. "Oh, Kath, honey—"

She did not understand the look on his face. "What is it, Uncle Tede? Has somebody been hurt? I was coming through the woods and I saw Cade in there, and he was down on the ground crying. He was in a terrible state—I couldn't get him to tell me what was the matter."

"Kath, it's Tiss. She was coming back in a wagon from the farm out there where she was staying. The farmer brought her in and when he stopped on the other side of the tracks she got down, waving to someone, and ran across even though the train was coming and her heel caught in one of the ties where it was split, and she didn't make it." Kath only stared at him and suddenly he grabbed her to him and she smelled the strong odor of cigar smoke and thought of how Aunt Maud didn't like it and tried to air the house. *Tiss! Tiss!* But nothing would come clear. She didn't understand. Did Uncle Tede mean that Tiss had been killed?

"Is she—is she gone, Uncle Tede?"

"Yes, Kath. She had high lace shoes on and couldn't get the lace undone, and the friend—the one she'd waved to and we think it must have been Cade—tried to help her and then had to run back. Kath, I'm glad she's gone, considering the way it happened."

He continued to hold her, and then his arms dropped but his hands still grasped her shoulders. Now Aunt Maud came toward them with the people she'd been talking to, and everybody went back along the street toward South Angela. Kath did not know what the people and Aunt Maud were saying. Sometimes Uncle Tede, who had an arm around her and would now and then draw her close and with his other hand reach over and briefly press her arm, said something, but she did not take it in. Gradually the other people must have dropped away, must have gone off along their own blocks, because after while Kath was aware that there were only the three of them. Aunt Maud, walking along silent on the other side of Uncle Tede, at last made some remark.

"What?" said Uncle Tede.

"I said, I guess she had it coming. I guess she's punished. You can't think but what, the way it turned out, it must have been the judgment of the Lord."

"Judgment!" burst out Uncle Tede. *"Punished! Who's* punished? Not Tiss. She's gone, she's out of it. But who's left? You know who's left. You know the one who's punished. And for what, I ask you? For what? So how do you figure?"

Aunt Maud stopped, staring straight ahead. "Yes," she said. "That's so, Tede. I never—"

"No, you didn't," shouted Uncle Tede, halting, glaring at her, seeming beside himself. "Because you think with your guts, an' that isn't thought. All your kind do, gossiping away down there in that front parlor, all you old bitten-back ones, married an' unmarried alike. Hattie's different. Maybe she's never known what it is to have a man take an'—"

Aunt Maud's arm shot out and she clutched the lapel of Uncle Tede's coat. "You don't dare to speak about my sister—"

Uncle Tede struck her off as if ridding himself of some noxious insect. "Yes, you old fool, I do—an' it's a compliment to her. Maybe Hat never bloomed under no man's hand, but she's never let herself get bitten back like you—talkin' about punishment an' the judgment of the Lord. My God! She'd maybe say Tiss did wrong—though what do we know about it?—but she'd have some knowledge of human nature an' some understanding that people do all sorts of things an' who knows what's the reason. She wouldn't be so stupid as to talk about God's punishment. What about people in floods an' earthquakes? What about the people in this war that's goin' on an' on, men an' women an' children who've never done a thing to deserve what they're goin' through? Are *they* being pun-

ished? You mean by the hundreds an' thousands, all in one
fell swoop? Who knows how things work, all crisscrossed an'
beyond our understanding? But you don't see that—you don't
stop to think about that. No, you go to church every Sunday
an' you put the finger of blame on this one and that one, just
as if you *know*, just as if you're Jehovah sittin' up there on
high and fit to judge—"

"But it's all there in the Bible!" cried Aunt Maud. "An'
you never read it. You've got too much else to do. Or maybe
you know too much to read it—maybe you know everything—"

"I don't know a goddamned thing. Only this—if I come in
late you're still up, waitin' for me, as if I was your husband,
an' you take on as if I'd been tomcattin' around all night, an'
you want to know everything I been doin', which would be
none of your damned business, when all I been doin' is talkin'
to some man over at the hotel, or walkin' Grant back over to
Willowtown when he's through work an' then wanderin' back
in my own good time an' having an all-out good smoke to
myself, just as I please. I'll tell you what, Maud, you're an
oppressor an' a blamer. You oppress both me an' Hat, an'
you're always blamin' us for something. Somebody's always
got to take the blame in your view, so you figure God's made
in your image an' likeness. You're a life killer, instead of a
life giver, an' I swear if one o' you has got to kick the bucket
before me, I hope it'll be Hat can stay on for a while, because
she's warm an' loving, not sharp and fault-finding like you.
An' if I have to take *care* o' one o' you, I pray to God it'll be
Hat, because I'd wait on that woman hand an' foot for all the
caring she's given me all these years, but I swear I'd grudge
every dish I lifted for you. I swear I'd be tempted to light out
like Clayton did if I had to live in that house alone with you,
an' I don't doubt but what I'd do it. Because without Hat to
lighten my days, I don't think I could make it."

Some way along, while Uncle Tede poured out his bitterness, Aunt Maud had stopped in the middle of the sidewalk and Kath and Uncle Tede turned. Her face had gone white, the lines drawn deep as if a finger had pulled them downward, and her pale eyes were fixed on his with a bleak sadness. And when he had finished, when he had uttered his last words, "Tede," she said, just above a whisper, "my own brother—"

"Oh, Maud!" he cried. "*Maud!* You go on home now. Just go on home—"

They were almost back at the house, and Uncle Tede took Kath's arm and they crossed the street to go up toward Main on the hotel side and Aunt Maud was left to go home alone.

When Kath and Uncle Tede got into the lobby, she saw Elizabeth Rule standing at the entrance to the dining room, and Uncle Tede nodded to Kath to go upstairs and he went over to Mama and slipped his arm through hers and said something to her and then they turned and went into her office. Kath stood at the foot of the stairs looking up at Arny, the little old bellboy, coming down. "Arny, where's Grant?"

He gazed at her in astonishment. "Grant!" he said. "Why, Miss Kath, what's the matter? You look terrible. Don't you remember—this is Tuesday—Grant's day off."

She went on upstairs and closed the door and sat in Mama's chair. And after a while Uncle Tede brought Elizabeth Rule in and she stood for a moment staring at nothing, then walked over to the middle of the floor as if she were blind and put her hands up to her face.

"I don't understand," said Uncle Tede to Kath. "What does she mean—what has *she* done? I took her into the office and when I told her what had happened, I thought she was going to faint. I've never seen anybody look like that. She sat down at the desk and she seemed to sort of fall forward onto it, her head on her arms, and she said, 'Oh, God, what have I done— what have I done—' But what did she mean? I don't see the connection. Can I get someone? Should I get Dr. Franklin? I think she needs help."

Kath got up and went to Elizabeth Rule and held her, but she did not move. She was shaking. "Mama, please lie down." Still she did not move. Perhaps she hadn't even heard. "Yes," said Kath, "yes, Uncle Tede, I think you'd better. Get Dr. Franklin."

17 🌿 Himself Unmoving

Elizabeth Rule lay on the bed whispering to herself, shaking from head to foot, her hands ice cold. But at last she was unconscious. Kath had taken her shoes off and put a blanket over her, and Dr. Franklin had given her a sedative. She would be unconscious until midnight, he said, and he would return then to see how she was and perhaps give her another. He had packed everything up again in his doctor's bag and stood at the foot of the bed looking at her in silence, and Kath had brought the desk chair over and was sitting close to the bedside. Uncle Tede had finally left. He would send Aunt Hattie, he said.

"What's happened to her, Kath? It seems more than grief—"

"But she loved Tiss. Tiss and Mama have been friends for years. Tiss did so much—"

"No," said Dr. Franklin, "there's something wrong, something terribly wrong. Your mother can't bear Tiss's death. She can't accept it. That's what I can't get at."

Kath looked away from him. "Maybe some day she'll tell you."

"So then there *was* something. I know my Elizabeth," he said, his entire attention fixed on that figure on the bed, and what he felt for Elizabeth Rule was plain in his face. He had no need to say anything. It was very embarrassing. "I think she must have told you I want to marry her. I would do anything for her. I would give her all the care and devotion she's never had—it's a crime her persisting in staying here in this place when there's no need—no need at all. We could be so happy, the four of us. You could have a brother and Danny would know the joy of having a mother for the first time in his life. My wife died when he was born—"

"I know," said Kath. "I was told. I've thought about that. I suppose it would be nice, Danny's getting a mother—"

Dr. Franklin's face, rather square, rather full, flushed pink. "*That* was not my purpose. That would be only a part. What I mean is, your mother could have a position of respect in this community—"

"Aunt Hattie said people already respect her."

"Oh, they do! They do! Everyone knows that. What I mean is, she could enjoy a very *happy* position. We would be a part of the Boughtridge circle together and it would make so much difference to me, to enjoy that with her. She is such a fine lady—I've never known a finer, never anyone like her." He stood there a little longer as if turning it all over, how his life could be changed, and then he sighed, picked up his bag, and went to the door. He would come back at midnight, he said. "Have you eaten anything, Kath?"

"But I don't want anything—I couldn't."

Well, he said, he would have something sent up, just in case.

When Kath, later, looked back on that time, it was all a confusion. Sometimes she was in bed trying to sleep, to escape thought, escape the unbearable pictures that came to her mind, or she would be sitting by the bedside still watching her mother's face (or did she dream this?). Sometimes Margaret

Jameson was there, or Aunt Hattie and Aunt Maud, or Uncle Tede or Dr. Franklin. Someone told her Herb had come by to ask for her. Perhaps it was the second night (had Dr. Franklin given her something, too?) that she woke when everything was dark and dead still and Elizabeth Rule was standing by the open window, looking down, and at once Kath was out of bed, wavering drunkenly across the floor and holding her from behind, both arms tight around her.

"Mama—don't—"

Elizabeth Rule stood quiet for a moment, then she took Kath's arms in both her hands and loosened them. She turned, touched Kath's face very lightly, and Kath remembered when she had done that to Aunt Lily when they were leaving the farm. "It's all right. I had nothing in mind. I was only standing here trying to catch hold, to steady myself, I was trying to think it all out—"

"And have you?"

Elizabeth Rule shook her head. No, she had not. Kath led her back to bed and after a while Dr. Franklin came again.

Afterwards, she could not be certain what was remembering and what was dream: Tiss and Grant happy to see her, always happy to see her, asking her to stay and eat with them, and they had their kind of food, not the kind Tiss could make for white people. (Kath begged Swan to make their kind and put it on the hotel menu—chitlins, greens cooked with pork and bacon, black-eyed peas and cracklins, and boiled pig's feet and tails and ears, and sweet potato pie—and he laughed till the tears came to his eyes and slapped his knee and asked her if she wanted him fired.) Tiss made molasses dreams, her own kind of cookie that nobody else knew how to make, and they had them for dessert and Grant teased her because she ate so many he said she'd never be able to roll herself home.

Grant telling her that when he was a little boy he would

go out with his father into the woods around Willowtown, thick, thick woods in those days, with deer and fox and possum in them, or out into the fields, and his father would whistle bird songs so true to each different kind, meadowlark and thrush, oriole and tanager and bobolink, that they would answer, and you couldn't tell, unless you were watching his father's lips, which was singing, his father or the bird. Grant tried to copy him, tried to vibrate his tongue while he whistled in that peculiar way that made the whistle come rippling and bubbling out, but he couldn't manage it and never had got the hang of it to this day.

When his father went into the woods, Grant said, he seemed to become a part of them and of the hidden, secret life there so that he could have called a deer to his gunsight as artfully as he did the birds to his call so that they answered him, but somehow he couldn't kill a deer. He would kill partridge and rabbit for food, but a deer—no. When Grant got a little older he was allowed to go with his father and the men on possum hunts and carry the "lightered"—a flaming torch, the resinous core of an old pine stump.

He couldn't whistle to the birds, but he could sing and he would go along through the woods with his father, singing the happiness that was in him because they were alone together in the wild, maybe picking flowers for the house, the mauve orchis pushing its head up through the dead leaves of thickets, or in spring and early summer, violets and spring beauties and wood anemones. So deep were his father's feelings for the woods and for all his natural surroundings that Grant could not help but be affected by him. Sometimes when he was working in the hay fields he would have to stand and listen to all that was going on, and he would start singing. Later he began singing in the church choir and had all these years ever since.

163

Tiss could sing, but not so that the bumps rose on your arms and you found it hard to breathe the way it happened when Grant let out his voice full force. She could dance, though, a buck and wing she said it was. And Grant and Kath would get her going with "Settin' on a Rail" and they'd clap along with it and Tiss's heels went faster and faster as the rhythm and the clapping speeded up until at last she flung herself on the bed gasping and laughing.

Tiss taking her to the movies down near the railroad station when she was younger, taking her into that black, queer-smelling interior (dust and sweat and dirty seat covers) somehow connected with sin because of the smell and the darkness and those incredible goings-on flickering across the screen that would get Tiss so wrought up she let out exclamations of warning to the hero when the villains were creeping up on him and the piano player thundered in the bass (used also for storms and battles and murder), or bursts of laughter over the comic parts, nervous laughter, high-pitched, as if Tiss were balanced on the edge of an emotion that could turn to grief in two minutes if someone died and the piece changed to "The Last Rose of Summer" or "The Two Grenadiers" or "Nearer My God to Thee." Because of the disturbing energy of Tiss's watching, people around them turned and angrily hushed her, but she paid no least attention and went right on laughing or exclaiming or weeping as if she were alone, though when the hero in armor walked straight into a burning castle and the flames engulfed him, she turned and grasped Kath to her bosom and pressed her face away because she knew that Kath, at the age of eight or nine, could not bear it.

Memory becomes dream in the night after Tiss is killed, and Tiss and Kath are in some theater in Columbus and Tiss gets up in the middle of the picture saying she has to go to the ladies' room, but never returns, and when Kath, at last, goes to find her, there is no one behind any of the doors and she goes outside to wait, but Tiss never comes and Kath has no way of getting back to South Angela nor even any money to phone, and it is night by now and Mama is waiting—with no word.

And this is dream, but true at the same time, that Kath steals a dime from Tiss but cannot spend it nor bear to look at her, and wakes in a sweat of guilt and misery because in her dream she opens Tiss's purse to put the dime back and Tiss sees her and thinks she is stealing. Must put it back, must get it back to her! Then remembers, lying there beside Mama in the early morning with the tears spilling, that she cannot ever return it to Tiss now, and that there is no need even to give it to Grant because she has given that dime back to Tiss years ago.

Tiss has gone. Where is she? How can a *being* vanish forever? Especially a being like Tiss?

"Kath, are you awake?"

"Yes, Mama—I'm here—"

"What happened?"

"Dr. Franklin gave you something to make you sleep."

"Yes—" and then after a pause, "Did we get up in the night? Was it last night I was standing at the window and you came to me because you were frightened of what I might do?"

"Yes, last night. Do you remember you were trying to think everything out, but couldn't?"

"And yet I believe I have. I have decided something." Kath waited for her to go on. "I have experiences, and I've always known when each one has come to an end. For me, they're like plants. They grow and come to flower, and die. And this one, here at the hotel, has died. I can't do anything more with it. It's finished. And there's another thing I know. I have got to talk to Grant quietly, here in this room or wherever he'll see me. Soon! If I never do another thing in this world, I have got to talk to Grant."

In the late afternoon of that same day Mr. and Mrs. Jameson took Elizabeth Rule and Kath out to Grant's. Mr. Boughtridge had told Grant that he would not be expected at the hotel for three days. And when they drew up in front of Tiss and Grant's, Elizabeth Rule got out and went a little way along the path alone, then turned. "I think that Grant would prefer it if you came too, Kath." Yes, he would. Whenever he had come up to their room with anything, with tea and toast in the afternoon on Elizabeth Rule's day off, or in the evening with their dinner when she wasn't feeling well, he would never come in but handed Kath the tray at the door. He had never once, in all the years they had lived at the hotel, entered their room.

There was a clear, cool fragrance in the air as they came along the path, and the smell of wet earth. Kath saw how black it was, freshly dug among the plants, not a weed to be seen, the dead blossoms picked away, the vines trimmed back, and all the leaves glistened so that Grant must just have watered. Only then, in this moment of noticing, did she remember how dusty and bedraggled and overgrown Tiss's garden had looked that day of the bonfire.

Now Lucky got up from where he'd been drowsing in the shade and moseyed over to shove his nose into Kath's hand and went up onto the porch with them. They stood at the door and knocked and Kath was frightened of how it would be, this meeting; of how Grant would look, of how he would talk to them, or be unable to. She did not know if she could bear to look at his face. And when she glanced sideways at Mama she saw the white line around her lips and saw the pleating on her blouse front going up and down. She looked ill and drawn with dark smudges under her eyes. Dr. Franklin hadn't wanted her to come, but she said she could not wait, that there would be nothing she could do with herself until she could talk to Grant and say all that was in her mind to say.

When Grant opened the door he appeared as he always had, except for his eyes, Kath thought. They were not the same, though the difference would have been beyond her explaining, for it was not simply a matter of sadness. "Mrs. Rule," he said. "Miss Kath—" and he stepped back, opening the door wide. "Please come in."

When they went in, Mama stood there looking up at him, her hands clasped in front of her. "I had to come. I can't tell you what I—" For a moment she had a struggle and turned away. "You see, this is something I've done, Grant—to the last person on earth I would have—"

"I know, Mrs. Rule, I know." He pulled two chairs forward. "Please sit down, you and Miss Kath," and he took a chair facing them. "I've been working in the garden. There isn't much you can do for the dead, but I thought it would be good to work with my hands. I could do that for Tiss—keep up the garden for her, and I could think. But never at any time in my thinking, Mrs. Rule, have I blamed you for what has happened. How could I? You brought me what you thought I needed, and that's all you did. Everything else was between Tiss and me and had nothing to do with you at all."

"Oh, Grant—*Grant*—"

"Mrs. Rule—"

"I acted out of concern," she burst out. "I wanted you to be happy, to realize what you could do, and I never once thought about Tiss. Except that I took it for granted that if you were happy, Tiss would be—"

"And I thought that I could reason with Tiss, but I couldn't. And she thought she could make me change my mind, but she couldn't. And that was the way it was between us, nobody being able to look ahead. How could we? How could you know at the time you brought the books how Tiss would take it? And who knows on what other day Tiss might have crossed those tracks, or at what time? She need not have been coming back from the farm. You're not guilty of anything, Mrs. Rule —you must not go on berating yourself. We have both of us got to see things as they are."

But how can you, Grant, see things as they are, when there are some things you don't know? But did he? For what had passed between Grant and Tiss was hidden, and perhaps this was what Kath could see in his eyes: the truth.

Now Grant, who had been glancing at Elizabeth Rule's face and away again, back and away, as one does in talking, allowed his gaze to meet hers and hold it for a moment, and Kath could not perceive what knowledge was exchanged, nor what unspoken feeling. And after a little, while Kath heard the doves in the linden tree outside repeating over and over, "Roo coo coo coo, roo coo coo coo," just as they had when Tiss was here, Elizabeth Rule spoke. "Yes, Grant," she said, "you are right, we have to see things as they are. But what I see is a succession of events that I started. And I know something now. Nobody can help me, not even you. It is something, this self-reproach, that has got to pass away, or lessen, and perhaps it never will. It isn't the words that are said—that Tiss might or might not have done this or that. It's what a person feels, and as for me, right now, there aren't any words that can change that. It's I who should be helping you, but I can't even help myself."

She told him then that they were leaving, and why; and as she and Grant talked and Kath looked at him as he sat there, his hands quiet in his lap and himself unmoving as he had been the whole time, suddenly Kath was six again and in the midst of two memories, one of the heat and one of the cold.

The first—the kind of day on which someone had told her

168

that a person could fry eggs on the sidewalk, but when she had gone and asked Swan for an egg and had broken it on the cement outside the hotel in the burning sun, all that happened was that its white had turned milky underneath, when she knew perfectly well that eggs frying in a pan sputter and pop and get that delicious crispy frill all around the edge. She waited a while, then knew she had been fooled and was furious and tried to rub away the disgusting runny pool with her sandal. Why did people say lies like that? And when she ran in and told Swan about it, he only laughed at her for being so stupid as to believe, and Grant got out a pan and fried two eggs with crisp frills, one for each of them, and laid them on buttered toast and they'd had a little feast right in the middle of the morning.

The second memory—a day of the first icy winter she and Mama were in South Angela when she stuck her tongue on the Boughtridges' iron fence and, finding she could not get it off, screamed and screamed, and Grant came and blew his warm breath between cupped palms in a steady stream on her tongue until she was able to bring it away, burning and tender. These were two of the first things he had done for her and she could not count all that he had done ever since.

"Grant," said Elizabeth Rule, "will you go on studying?"

"I must."

"And when you go away to law school and take the bar, then—"

"I'll come back. This is my place and the Willowtowners are my people. I'm going to come right back here."

"Write to me, Grant, won't you? I'll want to hear how you get on."

Later, when they stood on the porch and it came to Kath that she might not be seeing him again, all at once, without knowing in the least what she was about to do, she flung her arms around him, pinning his to his sides. "Good-bye, Grant," and she pressed her forehead hard against his chest. "I'll miss you—I'll miss you *very much*—"

He looked down at her, shaking his head. "I declare, Miss Kath," he said. "I declare!" And when she backed away and looked up at him, "You'll remember everything now, won't you? All the good times we had, you and Tiss and me. Those are the things you've got to hold to—"

18 🌿 Do You Remember?

Kath dear:

As a private celebration I went for a long walk this morning. Everything is so beautiful after the storm, the hills a rich soaked green, and I couldn't seem to contain myself with your mother's letter in my pocket, and had to get out and *go*. I kept thinking, as I walked, of that last early summer day you and I walked together when you kept asking, "What's *that*, Gran—and that, and that?" and I said Indian dipper, that pink one, and there's sweetbriar rose, and the orange one is butterfly weed, and the little blue one with the yellow center, forget-me-not, and that one there—that big yellow one—is the great mullein, and over there Indian paintbrush and purple bell-flower and black-eyed Susans. It's been so long, and you've changed so that I wouldn't know you if it hadn't been for the snapshots. Oh, but I would! And you're still my Kath, I can tell from your letters, despite a kind of queer constraint in your last two, as if you wanted to say so much more than you could. Your mother has told me about Tiss. What can I say, Kath? Nothing—nothing!

This isn't a very big house as you'll maybe remember, but there's room enough for each of us to have whatever privacy and solitude she desires. I believe in that. There are times when a person needs the company of herself alone. For some reason I've been low in my mind lately before I knew you were coming, and I've thought it's because the garden is thinning and the leaves dropping, turning yellow and mummy brown, and it was hottish and humid before the storm came— this melancholy in-between season just before October when the sky will lose its mistiness and turn a blazing blue and the trees will burn down the whole length of the valley. When it isn't spring I sometimes think I could live in an eternal October. Underneath my depression I of course knew what was the matter: the war, the never-ending war and the contrast between man and a world he doesn't deserve. Sometimes I love my solitude—and sometimes not, feeling useless, purposeless, when I completely lose my bearings and get panicky and the compass needle has to swing round to its true north again.

Now I'm steadied. The compass needle has stopped veering and I'm full of plans, knowing the iris must be cut and separated and the whole garden *got* after when I've finished the house. I was up in your eagle's nest this afternoon cleaning it out and getting it ready for you, washing the window and putting up fresh curtains and fresh linen on the bed. I'm afraid it will all seem terribly small to you now, Kath—just room for the cot and the dresser and a chair, but you loved it when you were four and were never in the least afraid to be up there alone in the dark and never wanted a candle or a lamp left burning and were especially happy when the moon was full and you could go to sleep in its light, that eerie flood pouring down through the open window. I even found myself wondering if I might not find a changeling in the morning.

I have the cot over there under the window now because I'm sure you're just the same. You always wanted to be outdoors. I think you're like me. The truth is, I feel very close to nature, rooted in it. It sustains me. To get my hands into the earth, that is my joy. My head is full of thoughts the whole day as I work, and the harder I work the faster the thoughts come until sometimes I have to be still for a moment to settle the matter with myself.

Not long ago you wrote me that you'd dreamed you looked down from a high mountain and saw me come out of the back door and shake a tea cloth, then gather it up and stand there for a moment looking all around. Kath, I've done that—exactly that, time and time again. How could you know? Do you remember me doing it?

And do you remember your room in the attic? You liked to stand there at the window and look out over the valley and tell me all the things you saw. There are many more houses now than when you were here. You and your mother are going to be surprised, but we're still a small town. If it gets big—I'm retreating into the hills. Soon it will all be as familiar to you as if you'd never left, and we'll walk our legs off, you and I, and your mother can rest. It will be good for her, to be quiet, to get back to her deepest self, to find herself again. Perhaps she will want to come with us on our walks after a while, but she must do whatever she likes. No burden of attachment will ever be laid on her. That is another part of my belief about privacy.

Just before you arrive I'm going to put flowers all over the house, cosmos and lavender and white asters, a few pink roses I have left, some day lilies and autumn crocuses, and the mums that smell of autumn. I want a big vase of flowers up on your dresser. Can you picture the steep pitched roof? Don't bump your head, which you couldn't possibly have done when you were small! Old Quince always comes up with me—just think, the little marmalade cat who arrived to live here just before you and your mother came all those years ago. My kind, comfortable companion, still as hale as ever, like his mistress.

Silly of me to write you this long letter when you'll be here in another week. But I wanted to, that's all. I had to talk to you. And now I'm going to say good-night—

From your loving Gran

19 ❧ To the Green Mountains

Mr. Boughtridge would not hear of Grant becoming manager of the hotel. Not at all suitable, he said, and he had someone else in mind. Grant was to continue as head waiter of the dining room, in which position he did very well. Jenny Knowles would become housekeeper. And Mrs. Boughtridge wanted to give a farewell tea for Elizabeth Rule.

"But I couldn't accept, Mrs. Boughtridge, thank you. Not after Tiss's death."

"Really not, dear?" The gracious smile faded. "Well, I'm sure we all extend our sympathies to poor Grant, but perhaps I don't quite—"

"She was a friend of mine, Mrs. Boughtridge, for all the years I've been here."

"Oh, I see." A questioning pause while Mrs. Boughtridge's smallish eyes trotted about over Elizabeth Rule's face as though trying to find a way in. Her own large face, red and beaded with damp, she kept pressing with a wisp of cambric. "Well, then," she said briskly. "I hadn't known. I *am* sorry, dear. We are very sorry to lose you—I'd only wanted to show some small appreciation, but under the circumstances I see we shall have to be satisfied with my intentions."

The room, now, was as it had been before Kath and Elizabeth Rule came to live in it, a hotel room merely in which, if Jenny Knowles chose to remain where she was, one traveling man after another would hang his pants and coat over the chair, put a few stray belongings on the dresser—his collar and collar stud, tie, watch and chain, a few folded bits of paper, his change—and gather them all up again the next morning and leave everything as bare and impersonal as before. And there was that mysterious bird who called in the early hours, Kath thought, but who would hear?

She folded her coat over her arm, picked up her bag, and looked at the ceiling. "Good-bye, dog," she said. There stood Mama at the door looking back at their room—that brown, shabby room in which Jason Rule had got down on his knees and wept—looking back with a proud and distant gaze as though already it were a part of the irrevocable past even before she had stepped out of it for the last time. She was shedding it. Thank God, was in her face. *Thank God.* "Well," said Kath, "we won't have to look at *him* anymore."

"Look at who?"

"At that poor old dog up there."

Elizabeth Rule glanced up. "I don't see any dog," she said and went out and along the hall.

So then he had existed for her alone and would perhaps never exist for anyone else. He had been her dog—that desperate, earless hound, forever fleeing as in a dream, making no progress, its neck stretched, lips drawn back in a grimace of terror, and the shapeless bird forever clutching its back. But fleeing from what, Kath had never finally determined, though she had told herself story after story in an interminable effort all these years to give shape and substance to that invisible pursuer.

Now Arny came and got the rest of their bags and she followed him into the hall and shut the door behind her.

176

The train for Columbus left at six in the morning and though Dr. Franklin had asked to drive them the five blocks to the station, Elizabeth Rule had had to tell him that the Jamesons had already offered and been accepted. But of course, he said, he would be there in any case to see her off. And there everybody was, beside the Jamesons and Dr. Franklin. Not Chattie—Chattie couldn't possibly be up at that hour of the morning, and besides she and Kath had said whatever they'd had to say the evening before—but Aunt Maud and Aunt Hattie and Uncle Tede, and Aunt Lily and Uncle Paul, so that Dr. Franklin had very little opportunity, much to his obvious distress, to say what was in his heart. He stood there, silent and balked, while Aunt Lily chattered, giving Mama instructions as to exactly what to tell Grandmother, and every now and then, when Aunt Lily turned away, he would murmur something to Mama in a low, sad voice, and she would answer courteously in a comforting, sensible, rather strained way. It was all a strain; she'd prayed for the train to come, she told Kath afterwards.

"—shall of course come up to see you one of these days, Elizabeth, if you wouldn't be averse—"

"But, no—not averse, Norris! Why should I be? Of course you may come—"

"Such an honor to know you. And my feelings won't change, my dear—my intentions, I mean. Please remember that."

"Oh, but I could never decide to live here again, in South Angela, Norris. I couldn't possibly. All this is over. You must understand."

He looked absolutely desolate.

And now Aunt Hattie and Uncle Tede moved closer, and Aunt Hattie said in a private voice, "Elizabeth, you wouldn't believe it, but something's happened to Maud. I don't understand—she's so quiet. I haven't had a jawing out in days."

Kath looked up at Uncle Tede and he slipped an arm around her shoulders and gave her a little shake.

"You be a good kid, now. You won't have your Uncle Tede to keep an eye on you." She could find no answer, and he tilted up her face. "Are you all right?"

"Yes—we went out to see Grant and I feel better. But it didn't help Mama." He said something to Elizabeth Rule and after a little Kath slipped around to Aunt Lily. "Aunt Lily, what about Pillow? Have you and Uncle Paul talked about him—about what's going to happen?"

"I didn't tell you, Kath. I haven't had a chance, what with all the upset. Pillow died last week. I guess he was quite a bit older when he came to us than I thought he was. I've somehow never thought much about his age. But you see, dear? What did I tell you and your mama? I prayed to God to take care of Pillow, and He has. Uncle Paul isn't going to have to decide about him now—he's safe. I *knew* it would turn out all right, and you remember that, Kath. If only I could make your mama see, it would have helped her all through this awful time. I can tell what a terrible thing it's been for her. You've only to look at her—she looks as if she's had pneumonia, though I'll have to admit I don't understand why it was quite so terrible. I mean, you'd almost have thought she'd lost you or me. But Elizabeth has always taken things so deeply. I don't understand her and never will. In some ways she's almost steely, and in others like a burning bush. Oh, Kath, if only she was a Christian I could be happy, but *that* I can do nothing about—"

There was Herb. She looked past Aunt Lily toward the station and suddenly he was standing there, behind it, right at the corner, where he had not been a moment before. She started toward him, heard the train whistle, far off, and began running. "Herb, where've you *been?* I thought you weren't coming—"

178

"I've been here, watching you. It was better that way."

"But, Herb, we could have been talking—"

"And what would we have said? No, it's better this way, to press it all into the last minute. I can't stand anything long-drawn-out. I just wanted to look at you. Kath, I got my letter—"

"Your letter?"

"Yes, the one from my uncle in England. He wants me to come, just as soon as possible. And I *will* go to Cambridge, if they'll let me in—but I'll see that they will—and live with Uncle Bob. He's as pleased as can be. He says he feels as if I'm his son, and I feel that way toward him, and here we've never even seen each other. So now it's all settled. And, Kath, I've decided something. I'll never have a family, never any ties, so I'm going to travel after I graduate. I'm going to see every corner of this world and I'm not going to stop until I have—"

"But, Herb, what will you do for money?"

"Earn it as I go—any old way, any way I can. I've never been anywhere, never even down to the southern part of this state to see the serpent of earth the Mound Builders made that's a quarter of a mile long. But I'm going to see it—and I'm going to see you up in Vermont before I go to England—Kath, I'm just rattling on because I don't want you to leave. What'm I going to do now, with you gone? You've got to write to me—"

"You know I will—"

"So I'll have yours and Uncle Bob's letters. And that's all I'll have, and looking forward to seeing you one day, maybe in a year or two—"

"But you've got to save—"

"I know. But I'll manage. Maybe I could ride the freights. Kath, here's the train—you've got to go now. Your mother's calling—"

Their arms went around each other and they held on, and then without looking at him again, she turned and ran.

The telephone wires rise and fall, rise and fall, each rise catching up a new scene, the green waves of hills with their grazing cattle, the patches of woodland, the fields where the men are working, and each fall letting it go. She hears the song of the wheels and marks the hollow sound every time they cross a cutting, and is filled suddenly, in spite of everything, with a moment of the old ecstasy at the thought of seeing Grandmother—soon, soon now—and the green mountains at last. But I have no right to be happy. I will think of Tiss.

"We have no right to be happy ever again, have we, Mama?"

"But we will be. That's what's treacherous—saving and betraying. We will be."

They pass the road to Uncle Paul's that she has not seen since that late golden afternoon when the shadows of trees were drawn long across the landscape, and the pony cart was being swept, as if fatefully marked out for destruction, into the path of the approaching train as it hurtled toward them under the overarching sky in which swallows were skimming, sketching out, with swift strokes of their arrow-shaped bodies, intricate designs against the untroubled blue and calling to each other with plaintive cries. Now it is early morning and the shadows of trees are drawn long in the opposite direction across the shorn fields as the train bears them away and away, out into the rolling open countryside to which they will never return.